SOUL FOOD

Novel by LaJoyce Brookshire

**Written and Directed by
George Tillman, Jr.**

SOUL FOOD

Novel by LaJoyce Brookshire

**Written and Directed by
George Tillman, Jr.**

HarperPaperbacks
A Division of HarperCollins*Publishers*

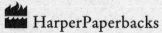 HarperPaperbacks

A Division of HarperCollins*Publishers*

10 East 53rd Street, New York, N.Y. 10022-5299

ISBN 0-06-101298-X

HarperCollins®, 📖®, and HarperPaperbacks™ are trademarks of HarperCollins*Publishers,* Inc.

Cover artwork courtesy of Twentieth Century Fox Film Corporation

Insert photos by Chuck Hodes

First printing: October 1997

Printed in the United States of America

Visit HarperPaperbacks on the World Wide Web at http://www.harpercollins.com

❖ 10 9 8 7 6 5 4 3 2 1

For My Mommie Jo (Joana Baker)
back in Chicago, who all of my life
has given *me* plenty of food for my soul.

ACKNOWLEDGMENTS

There are a few in my life whom without their unconditional love and endless support this project would have never come to fruition:

—My Father in Heaven who enlightened with divine inspiration daily.

—My husband Gus who allowed me to miss making meals and creep out of bed in order to make deadlines.

—My son Tony who kept me and the dogs fed when I forgot to feed them and myself.

—My blessed literary agent Marie Brown who is my Fairy Godmother.

—My Executive Producer of the "Woman of the Week" show, Miss Lucille Hubbard.

—My prayer warriors— Mayla Billips, Lencola Sullivan, Mama Brookshire, Susan Ellis, Terria Ladner, Nina Lynn Billips, Arlene McGruder, Peri Golightly, Theara Ward, Claudette Dyches, Anna Maria Bishop, James Ellerby, Elder Sam Williams, Reverend Kenneth Pearman, E. Lynn Harris, George Howard, and Zee.

—My wonderful editors Peternelle van Arsdale and Kristen Auclair.

—And finally, my best friend in the whole wide world, Theresa Gibbs who listened patiently as I read pages over the phone long distance.

Thank you all. I only hope to continue to be a beacon of light.

FOREWORD

I can remember those Sunday dinners at my grandmother's house like it was yesterday. It was a tradition for my family and many black families I knew while growing up in Milwaukee during the '70s and '80s.

I was raised by my mom, six aunts, and a strong grandmother who were strict about family members showing up for those dinners. I can see them now in that hot kitchen, cooking and gossiping at the same time like it was a work of art. There would be special dishes like dressing, candied yams, black-eyed peas, tea cakes, fried chicken, dumplings, egg pie, and sock-it-to-me cake. My five cousins and I would snack in the kitchen and go for the cake bowl so we could lick the mix. Damn, it tasted good.

While the women were cooking, the men—my dad and uncles—would be in the living room watching the games. They were either discussing who was the best fighter between Ali and Foreman, or the latest Ford or General Motors car that was coming out.

Those Sunday dinners weren't just limited to family. Neighbors would drop by to get some of my grandmother's cooking. The reverend of our church was a regular, and we even had homeless religious fanatics who would come in predicting the end of the world. My grandmother would give a plate to anybody who came by.

I remember the talent shows my cousins and I would perform for the grown folks. The barbecue cook-outs. The family reunions. The Christmas grab bags. The big Thanksgiving dinners when extended member from nearby states would visit. Those times were precious. As I grew older and went away for college, things changed. Times changed.

When the mid '90s approached, my family began to drift apart. Kids left for college. Elders passed away. There were marital disputes and sibling rivalries. The suburbs became real and family members were moving away from one another. And eventually, there were no more Sunday dinners. I'm twenty-eight years old now, and I miss those days.

Creatively, everything fell into place for me making *Soul Food*. Because I spent one year writing the script, I knew every shot in my head before I shot the film. And from the beginning, my wife was there giving me support and input on the dailies from the film. I had very experienced actors who brought what I had on paper to life. The most brilliant music producer of our time, Kenny "Babyface" Edmonds, was on my team and producer Robert Teitel was there to watch my back, along with producer Tracey Edmonds.

On the other hand, making *Soul Food* was the hardest thing I have achieved in my young life. My grandmother died midway through production, and it was a real setback for me. But as I continued to make the film I remembered an important line from the movie: "If you let the bad things stop you, then you won't be here for the good things." Then I realized the significance of *Soul Food*. What it meant and how those dinners kept individuals and family together. We must continue our traditions and rituals. We must continue to socialize and eat together. This unity is what's missing today. I wanted to make a film that celebrates family and, at the same time, explores why families break apart. I wanted to make a film where everyone everywhere—young or old, black or white—would be able to relate, reminisce, and learn. So we can bring the good times back. Because it's the soul food that is feeding us and constantly forcing us to grow.

—George Tillman, Jr.
Chicago, 1997

SOUL FOOD

1

SPORTING A NEW PAIR OF NIKES, THE LATEST trendy clothing, and a well-groomed haircut, Ahmad Simmons strolled casually down the hospital corridor carrying a dozen roses. At ten years old, he was not the ordinary kid. Ahmad had seen and heard plenty. Maybe even a little too much. Other ten-year-olds couldn't be so bothered with the things that affected him. With sick people on all sides, the walk en route to room 226 left him unfazed. Ahmad's focus was on remaining calm. He kept pushing down deep the emotion he felt for his loved one lying there in the hospital, emotion to be released in the quiet place he reserved for when he needed a good cry. He had always been able to keep his feelings under control by thinking out loud to himself. Somehow, it helped him process things a ten-year-old really shouldn't have to feel.

Ahmad turned to enter the room, but suddenly could not bring himself to go any further than the doorway. His ears were tuned in to the humming, beeping, and ticking emanating from all of those contraptions. Even though there was the average hospital chaos going on in the hallway, this room had a tranquillity that magnified every sound. Frozen in the same spot, absorbing the vision, it finally registered with Ahmad that this was indeed serious. Faced with the ugly reality before him—his loved one lying there motionless—Ahmad's mind floated off to a time three months ago when everything was all good.

Ahmad hated the rented tuxedo. It felt like someone had sent the penguin suit he had been forced to wear to the cleaner's and requested heavy starch just to torture him.

Ahmad managed to smile anyway, because for his family, this was a joyous occasion. His aunt, Robin "Bird" Joseph-Davis, had jumped the broom with Lem Davis.

Ahmad watched Aunt Bird and his new Uncle Lem. They looked so happy. The true blushing bride, Bird had money pinned all over her wedding gown during the money dance. Standing at the edge of the dance floor, Ahmad had been waiting for the opportune time to walk up to his aunt and pin onto her dress the money he had been holding. The reception was packed with a variety of dressed up people, many he had never seen before.

Mother Joe saw the flash of frustration that crossed the little man's face and gently led him toward the bride. Still unsure about the timing of pinning the money, he looked back at his Big Mama, who gave him a reassuring wink that he was doing the right thing. Called Mother Joe by everybody else, she was always Big Mama to Ahmad, and she was the rock of the Joseph family. Slowly, Ahmad went over to Bird and pinned on the twenty dollar bill. He knocked fists with his new Uncle Lem and Bird bent down to kiss him.

Aunt Robin was Mother Joe's youngest,

and everyone called her Bird. Ahmad didn't know much about her new husband, Lem, except that folks were always doggin' him out, because he had been in jail.

At twenty-two, Bird was the owner and operator of her very own beauty salon, and the Joseph family was downright proud of their baby girl. Lem, a street savvy individual who had recently gotten out of jail, could claim a few things as well: great sense of humor and a job that was neither too stable nor worth discussing. But most of all, he loved him some Bird. And that, if nothing else, was his card of acceptance from the rest of the family.

Raising three girls by herself after the death of her husband, Mother Joe was held in high esteem by everyone she met. A robust, mahogany woman with a hearty, infectious laugh, she dished out worldly wisdom as easily as she breathed. She was so irresistibly lovable that people found themselves completely entranced by her inviting spirit. Ahmad's mother always told him that his grandmother had never made one enemy in her whole life, and if she did, she'd have them over for some of her smoked ham or deep-dish peach cobbler and they'd be down with her after that.

On this wedding day of her youngest, Mother Joe was doing triple duty as the mother of the bride, cook, and server, and she would have it no other way. There was a long line of people anxiously waiting to dig into Mother Joe's renowned soul food fixin's. She had prepared all of the favorites. Collard greens, fried chicken, yams, rice and beans. And there was plenty! Enough to fill up four long tables. Enough even for the hungry tribe in attendance. The decked-out folks were not only gathered at this wedding to wish the couple well; for sure, Mother Joe's cooking was more than an added attraction.

One guest was particularly ecstatic over the food: the trash-talking, street pimp–looking, ever roving-eyed Reverend Williams. No sooner had Mother Joe handed him a full plate than he'd be back for more, his mouth still full of macaroni and cheese. It was a testament as much to Mother Joe's fantastic fare as to the Reverend's greed.

He soon took his third plate and commented, "Mama Joe, I tell you, this soul food is great, and this sure is a great wedding."

"Thank you, Reverend," she gushed.

"And the daughters are lookin' good, too," he said, licking his fingers. "Especially that Lady Bird. I asked her would you marry the Reverend? She said, 'Reverend, if I marry you, then I got to have sex every night.' I said, 'Okay, then put the Reverend down for Tuesday.'" He chuckled and dutifully planted a kiss on Mother Joe's cheek before he joined the other guests stuffing their faces.

Several couples took advantage of the good music to shimmy away the calorie-laced meal. Ahmad saw everybody on the floor whooping it up, including his eight-month pregnant mother Maxine, wearing her bridesmaid dress, and his dad, Kenny. Maxine was the family's middle child. Being a supporting wife and a loving mother were her sole priorities, and Ahmad and his eight-year-old sister, Kelly, were good examples of the emphasis Maxine placed on her children. Ahmad hoped that whoever that was in the oven would get here in a hurry. He had eavesdropped on his mom and dad and heard talk that the baby was a boy. He definitely wanted another man around—not just to play with, but to also help raise.

Ahmad spotted his Aunt Teri dancing with her husband Miles—like Miles Davis. Ahmad knew they were both lawyers and had big-time dough. The oldest of the Joseph sisters, Teri was also a bridesmaid. She was the family success story—beauty, brains, and plenty of money. Teri was self-assured and extremely mindful of her success. In fact, Teri's success meant far more to her than her beauty, although she had looks that could win her the title of Miss America. Her husband Miles was equally confident. He was Fine with a capital "F," really cool and confident, with a great build and distinguished gray hairs.

As Bird and Lem moved their way around the dance floor, a well-dressed black man named Simuel St. James sauntered up to Bird and flashed a one hundred dollar bill at her with a sexy smile. Simuel pinned the hundred to her dress. Slowly and deliberately, as if there was no one else in the room, he slid his fingers across her chest, feeling up the bride right out in the middle of the dance floor. He grinned suggestively at Bird and nodded to Lem, who somehow missed the implication of the entire episode.

Lem may have missed it, but Teri and Maxine, glancing at one another, clearly did not. The blushing bride turned red beneath her honey-brown glow. Forcing a smile at her husband, she left him on the dance floor and ran for the ladies' room. The music changed from slow to fast, and a convivial woman in a tight dress took advantage of Bird's absence to sashay up to Lem and request a dance in far too friendly a fashion. Maxine and Teri were too through with this public display of poor taste—and from such a trashy-looking guest. Still passing plates, Mother Joe saw it too. She would. She never missed a thing.

In his sloppy drunkenness, Lem did not seem bothered a bit by the woman's raunchy moves. Miss Thing was clearly enjoying her position as center-stage attraction with the groom. She proceeded to move his hands to her butt to the beat of the music. Family members and guests were now all watching in embarrassment. Infuriated, Maxine and Teri headed toward the bathroom. Mother Joe sensed trouble.

Ahmad and some of his little friends and cousins were enjoying the show, laughing at Lem and looking at the woman wiggle her butt. They slapped high fives like Lem had it going on. Mother Joe stared Ahmad down. Sensing the wrath of Mother Joe, the other boys scattered. They, too, knew better.

"Who's Big Mama's favorite grand-baby?" she questioned.

"Me." Ahmad beamed proudly, because not only was he the favorite grandbaby, but also the first.

"What will my Sweet Pea do for Big Mama?"

"Anything," he said with pure adulation.

"Then find your Aunt Bird and tell her to get her butt out here with her new husband now!" she ordered.

The three sisters had locked the door and convened a meeting in the ladies' room. A crowd had gathered to hear the commotion going on inside. Ahmad pushed through and pounded on the door. Maxine opened the door and looked down on him peeking through his fingers.

"Bird!" he yelled past his mother. "Big Mama said get your black ass out here!"

Maxine flipped. "Boy, Mother Joe ain't told nobody to get no black ass nowhere! Now stay outta grown folks business!" She slammed the door in his face. Ahmad just blinked and gave a "well-don't-shoot-the-messenger" shrug.

Bird paced back and forth pulling, the money off her dress. "I mean, who invited Simuel," she yelled. "*I* didn't."

"It's not about that," Teri interjected. "It's about your man not doing a damn thing while the boy's feelin' you up like a tomato."

"And he's out there with some Miss Thing bumping and grinding like there wasn't a wedding ten minutes ago," Maxine informed.

Bird went to the door, took a look, and freaked. "That's Tomeka. His ex!" she exclaimed mortified.

Maxine was fit to be tied. She couldn't believe that Bird has married this piece of trash. "See, I knew this would happen," she steamed while looking in the mirror and powdering her face. "Drag some no-money-havin', no-job-havin'—"

"He does too have a job!" Bird defended.

"—No-place-havin' convict in here, marry him, then put him on family," Maxine huffed.

Teri joined her at the mirror, and they continued to talk as if Bird was not there. "Her *family*? Oh no. He's on *me*," she coolly reminded Maxine. "I paid for this wedding. I flew his convict ass up here from Joliet."

Maxine was boiling. She did not care who paid for what. "Why you always got to go there?" she demanded. This was not the time for Teri to bring up what she had paid for again. Maxine was furious, and as if in response, she felt the baby kicking.

Clutching her stomach, she grunted to Bird, "Well, I hope the boy is kickin' it in the bedroom, 'cause he got the baby kickin' in here."

"It won't change," cried Bird, sinking into a chair. "You guys will never like him. Everything he does is wrong. Everything I do is trifling."

Teri eased up a little, realizing that they had made their baby sister feel so defeated on her wedding day. True, Bird had made several bad choices in life, and her choice in men ran number one on that list. However, this was not the time. "No girl," she consoled, snuggling her little sis to her bosom, "we don't want to start trouble on your wedding day." Lem did not exactly meet the Joseph criteria for marriage, but Bird was wildly in love with him. They couldn't argue with that. Teri saw the disappointment cross Bird's face, and it upset her.

"I just . . . we want you to have the best," Teri managed to say without further inflicting her misgivings on the situation.

Bird was resilient as ever, "But I do have the best. Can't you be happy for me?"

Teri felt ashamed of herself for casting a moment of uncertainty on this happy day. And Bird did not hesitate to place the pointed question to her directly.

Maxine came out of the stall and wiped her brow with a Kleenex, "Look, if you're happy, we're happy," she announced while seeking confirmation from Teri. "So I say we go out there and beat the 'ho down."

They all laughed at first, because Maxine had always been the most crazy and aggressive of the three. The Joseph sisters might not have seen eye-to-eye on a lot of things, but they had stood united fist-to-fist on more than one occasion. They were not afraid. In fact, they could not care in the least that they were all beautifully dressed— with one in a wedding gown—and one very pregnant. Their chief concern was that the baby of their family was in the process of being violated by some chick at her very own wedding. When they finished laughing, it took only a second to think seriously about Maxine's proposition and storm out of the bathroom in sisterly union, ready for real action.

A crowd was gathered around the dance floor, rooting and applauding. The ladies pushed through to the front and, to their surprise, found the center of attention was not Lem and his ex, but Lem and Mother Joe "cutting a rug."

The music was a hip-hop number, and Lem could barely keep up with Mother Joe, who was swift and light on her feet in spite of her size. She was wiggling her hips, imitating the latest dances. It was clear to all that Mother Joe must have watched *Soul Train* every week to keep up with the dances like that. The crowd was clapping and keeping beat.

Smiles slowly crossed each of the sister's faces as they watched their mother dance with the spirit of a young woman. She danced with the same vigor with which she plunged into life. None of them knew she could still move that way. Soon the girls were moving in rhythm with their mother. The song came to an end, and Lem and Mother Joe hugged. Each embrace signified a bond—for Lem, it meant thanks for showing me I'm welcome in the family; for Mother Joe, it said welcome to the family, because our baby loves you. The guests went wild.

Ahmad grinned from ear to ear at his Big Mama. Mother Joe winked at him. He winked back. Grandma was the only one who kept the family together, no matter what, he thought to himself. He loved her to death.

2

STILL STANDING IN THE THRESHOLD OF THE hospital room, Ahmad was deep in thought. Finally, he entered and silently placed his flowers on a table. Then he took a seat in the chair next to the hospital bed. He looked down at the frail woman lying there close to death.

Mother Joe, her strength and vigor gone. He looked down at her feeble body. One of her legs had been amputated and bandaged. He tried to be strong, but he was really still a little boy, and the emotion rose to the surface at last.

◯   ◯   ◯

Mother Joe moved about the yard with
vigor as she plucked various herbs and vegetables from the ground for three-year-old
Ahmad. The Victorian house had a lovely
yard, and it was beautified by her wonderful
green thumb. Tomatoes, cabbage, greens,
and every herb from thyme to sage burst
from the ground in abundance.

She carried her pickin's into the house
and plopped them into a pot of boiling hot
water on the stove. Mother Joe tossed in a
pinch of this and a shake of that and stirred
the mixture. When the combination had
simmered down and gotten soft, she poured
the murky green liquid called pot liquor
into a glass. It was a known fact, passed
down from the days of slavery, that the liquid from a combination of herbs and vegetables had the power to cure ailments and
diseases. She took the glass over to Ahmad,
playing with his toys. He fought her after
smelling it and frowned a "this-sure-is-
nasty-are-you-sure-I-have-to-drink-this"
frown. Mother Joe gave him a look. Ahmad
nodded and drank the medicinal remedy.

Later, the Joseph family sat enjoying
a delicious Sunday meal. Everyone was in

attendance, including the Reverend.
Mother Joe stared beyond her dinner guests
and looked dreamily at little Ahmad. Never
in her life had she been daunted by anything
that a doctor had said. Not about herself or
her children, and she certainly would not
hear of the doctor's predetermining that her
first grandbaby would never walk.

With Ahmad as her focus, Mother Joe
slowly got up from the dinner table and
went to where he was playing in the living
room, cooing at him all the while. Mother
Joe was convinced that he was going to
walk that day. She lured him to her with a
toy and took a step back to give him distance. The dinner conversation went silent.
Everyone painfully watched Mother Joe
encourage him. They were all too familiar
with the doctor's prognosis and Mother
Joe's lack of faith in it. Ahmad was born
premature, and there were major complica-
tions with his delivery that forced an emergency surgery. As a result, Maxine and
Kenny were told their newborn would
never walk. Emotionally torn between the
medical analysis of Ahmad's future and
Mother Joe's abiding faith in God, the family had taken an unspoken stand somewhere
in the middle as not to offend God or

Mother Joe. But Ahmad was now three and still had not walked. Maybe the doctors were right.

Maxine left her seat at the table and tried to come to her child's rescue.

"Mama, don't," she pleaded. "Don't do this."

"Hush up. My baby is going to walk today," she said, smiling at the child. "Aren't you, sweetie? Come to Big Mama," she encouraged, holding the toy out to him. "Come on."

Little Ahmad turned to his grand-mother, focusing intensely on her eyes. Mother Joe's stare was so friendly and invit-ing that he tried only to stumble and fall. Maxine moved toward him to help, but Mother Joe admonished her to keep her place. Maxine knew that when her mama had her mind made up to do something, it could be considered done. Ever since they were little girls, that was the way it had been. But now, watching her own child struggle brought tears to her eyes. Maxine wasn't so sure if the tears were for the pain of her child or the frustration in watching her mama silence her and take charge of her son.

Mother Joe and Ahmad locked eyes. It

was almost as if her eyes were the will for him to try. Bit by bit, he lifted himself to his feet. "That's my baby," Mother Joe continued to encourage. "Come on . . . come on."

Shaky and unsteady, he finally moved one leg toward Mother Joe. She moved back with the toy to entice him further, and then he stepped again toward her outstretched hand.

The family members gasped, and Maxine now cried a mother's tears of pure joy. Mother Joe and the family begin clapping and cheering for the baby, and Maxine held him for dear life. But it was Mother Joe whom Ahmad looked to for approval. She gave him a beaming smile.

Ahmad and Mother Joe had been connected by an unspoken bond ever since. They could communicate without saying a word out loud. The family knew this bond existed between the two and called it their ESP thing.

Ahmad inherited Mother Joe's deep love and sense of loyalty to family. His favorite memories were of Sunday dinners spent at his Big Mama's house. In Mississippi, the older folks would get together after church to talk smack and chow on some good soul food. Mother Joe kept the tradition going after she and her husband moved to Chicago.

The dinner scene was always the same. Occasionally, there would be a dinner guest or two, but always those in attendance would be in a great mood, laughing and socializing—Maxine, Kenny, Bird, Teri, Miles, Reverend Williams, Ahmad, Kelly, and Mother Joe.

The atmosphere of the Joseph home was warm and inviting. It was surrounded by family history documented in several photographs, including one of Grandfather Joseph and Mother Joseph on their wedding day more than fifty years ago. Grandfather Joseph owned a barbershop and a corner store, as well as a Laundromat. He never believed in working for anyone else but himself. It was said that he knew his whole life that the only jobs he would ever have would be only those he created, because, in his mind, black people had already worked hard enough—for free—for others to last all eternity. His thought toward business fueled a family rumor: Word was that Mother Joe stashed a lot of the money he had made someplace, because she did not believe in banks. But no one dared to ask her about it directly—not even Ahmad.

Other photos were of Maxine and Kenny's wedding and one from Teri's graduation from Northwestern Law School. She graduated in the top of her class.

As with most things that were a mainstay in the home, the photos were taken for granted and rarely noticed anymore. Everyone was always too busy digging into the food and having a great time. Sometimes they would have contests to see who could eat the most. It seemed that Reverend Williams always won. And after consuming more food than anybody else, he would excuse himself, grab a few pieces of chicken, and motion for a plate to go. The man had no shame.

On his way out, he kissed all of the women in the house. Kenny and Miles hated to see the Reverend kiss their women good-bye. Maxine, Teri, and Bird tried to avoid kissing the Reverend on the lips, but he skillfully made lip contact with them anyway. He got plenty of practice, and he enjoyed every second of it. Kenny fumed. He knew Maxine and her sisters didn't like the slickster Reverend slobbering all over them. Their distaste for him was 100 percent apparent; they only tolerated him for their mama.

A photo on the piano was of a family member whom the children only knew as the old man upstairs. Uncle Pete had not left his room in ten years. The photo showed no signs of such eccentricity—in it, young Mother Joe and her older brother Pete were holding up a newly caught fish. They stood at the edge of the river smiling ear to ear at their catch.

When it came to her brother, Mother Joe dismissed his habits with a "lights on, nobody's home" comment that everybody understood. Every day, Mother Joe set a food tray in front of Uncle Pete's bedroom door. The ritual was always the same: His door would slowly open and nothing but a walking cane would protrude from inside of the dimly lit room to slide in his meal.

One Thanksgiving, Ahmad and Kelly were adamant about getting a glimpse of the old man they had only seen in photos. When his tray was put in front of the door, they waited quietly in the hallway until the door opened to retrieve his meal. Then they ran to the room and Ahmad put his foot in the door to prevent it from closing. Young

Ahmad yelled out in pain as it repetitively closed on his foot until he removed it. Finally, Kelly and he watched the door slam shut in their faces. The message was clear: Uncle Pete did not want to be bothered, and Ahmad and Kelly should have known better.

Ahmad laughed out loud when he thought of those good old days . . . before it all went bad.

T HE CHURCH BELLS IN THE DISTANCE PLAYED
a sweet serenade that was an audible relief
to the residents of the South Side of
Chicago. Its cadence could be heard for
miles. Several new-model cars parked outside of Mother Joe's, indicating that her vis-
itors had plenty for which to be thankful:
Teri's and Miles's Range Rover, Maxine's
and Kenny's new Integra, Lem's used—but
in good condition—Bronco, Reverend
Williams's white Cadillac.

Dinner was about to be served at the

Joseph house, and the guests diligently waited with delectable anxiety for the meal being prepared.

Less patient was Reverend Williams, who already had his napkin tucked into his shirt; he made no apologies for the reason why he had come this—and all other—Sundays. Barely containing himself, he engaged in a bid whist game with Kenny and Lem while watching football. Miles entertained everyone by playing the old piano in Mother Joe's living room.

Music was Miles's secret passion. Sure, he was a successful lawyer with a beautiful, successful wife, but it was music that really moved his soul. He loved coming to Mother Joe's on Sunday just so he could play that piano. It may have been old, but it still had a good sound. He began a rendition of "My Girl," and Ahmad sang and danced with the beat. The ten-year-old knew the words to the song and even how to do the Temptations walk along with it. It was a funny sight to see. A youngster with such an old soul.

Teri hovered in the doorway to the kitchen, and her blood began to boil. He made her so mad practicing his music. What did it mean, anyway? And didn't he have some cases that he could be using this valuable time to work on instead of fiddling around with that damn piano? As far as she was concerned, he was wasting his time. This subject was a particular sore spot in the continuing saga of Teri and Miles. He was convinced that she didn't want him to play music because it made him happy. And she was convinced that he played music just to make her mad. .

Everyone else was clearly enjoying the music. Seeing him with an appreciative audience irritated Teri even further. She stormed back into the kitchen, fully intending to have a talk with her man later about making such a spectacle of himself in front of her family.

The well-lit kitchen might as well have had a neon sign blinking above the door that said "Mother Joe's Cooking Laboratory." It was a complete working environment—every chef's dream. There was an old gas stove with the griddle atop the range from the 1950s that Mother Joe adamantly refused to have replaced. Over the stove hung all types of utensils for easy access while cooking. Good chefs had their most-used items within arms reach, and Mother Joe was no exception. Bird and Maxine wore aprons and were working up a sweat at the center isle. Mother Joe, too, had donned her appropriate kitchen attire: full chef's apron with a scarf wrapped around her head to sop up the sweat of her labor.

Each of them had a task to complete for the meal. Over the years, they had developed a rhythm that sped along the dinner process. Mother Joe cut up chicken for frying. Teri iced the chocolate cake. Maxine stripped stems from collard greens. Bird stirred up the fish cake dough. The women worked in tandem with a comfortable silence between them.

Mother Joe took a seat at the workstation and began to put flour in a paper bag for the chicken. She glanced around the kitchen at her girls, half monitoring their cooking assignments, half reflecting on their lives. She loved these moments when they all worked together. Nothing else warmed her heart so.

After Maxine had finished cleaning them, Bird stirred the greens and measured one quarter cup of Lawry's Seasoned Salt to pour into the pot. Mother Joe jumped up in the nick of time to save them. "Ooh, no baby, that's too much," she admonished lovingly. "Just throw about four pinches in there," she said, doing it herself. Even though Lawry's Seasoned Salt was a cooking staple that replaced white salt, Mother Joe knew that too much could ruin the pot.

Bird frowned. "Now mama, how you know how much to put in there without using a measuring cup?"

Maxine and Teri shook their heads at Bird. The cooking thing was something she had yet to master.

"And why we got to eat ham hocks, anyway?" Bird suddenly demanded to know.

Mother Joe looked at her youngest baby knowingly and, without giving her the "you just know" routine, she patiently explained. "Well, back in slavery, that was all we had to eat," she began while shaking the chicken pieces in the paper bag with seasoned flour. "Ham hocks and neck bones, pig's feet and chitterlings. And we just learned how to make it all taste good by trying things. You see, soul food is about cooking from the heart."

"That's right Mama," Maxine agreed as she moved on to boil the potatoes, which she would later mash.

Bird listened to her mother and continued to stir the greens. "Okay, then try this," she stated proudly, lifting the ladle for her mother's approval.

Mother Joe took a taste and smacked her lips discerningly to decide the missing flavor. "Put another pinch in there," she ordered, commending Bird at the same time for its near perfection.

Bird smiled and added the pinch of seasoning salt as told. Then she moved to her next duty—the macaroni and cheese. For many soul-food connoisseurs, the macaroni and cheese was the icing on the cake, the sweet potato to the pie, the barbeque to the chips. The mac and cheese had to be slammin' or the entire meal was declared a disaster.

With that much stock put in one dish, thank God for Bird that the mixture was already prepared. She simply had to pour it into the pan that would go into the oven. Then it would bake until just a bit crusty around the edges and golden brown on top.

Maxine was making intricate cut marks in the ham for the insertion of cloves while bopping to the music. "Ooh, that music is sure sounding good out there."

Teri, dicing sweet potatoes for the pie, commented snidely, "If Miles paid as much attention to his cases as he does to his music, we could both retire tomorrow."

"Now, now," interjected Mother Joe, coming to Miles's defense while putting the chicken into the sizzling hot grease, "God gave Miles two things he does well. Music and the law."

"Please, mama. There's no future in music," Teri stated, agitated that she had to even have this conversation about her husband. She continued to cream butter, nutmeg, and brown sugar into the sweet potato mixture. "Every musician I know can barely eke out a living," Teri insisted.

"Well, I think he sounds good," Maxine threw in, bringing the conversation back to where it began.

Teri sucked her teeth a bit and glared a look of betrayal at her sister, "You would."

The swinging kitchen door cracked open and Lem peered into the room in search of Bird. He saw her, grinned, and whistled out a very suggestive, "Pssst."

Bird grinned back as she gave her sisters an "I'm-sure-you-all-will-take-care-of-the-rest-of-this" look. Wiping her hands, she took off her apron and sauntered out of the kitchen with Lem.

"Newlyweds," teased Maxine, finding it amusing.

Teri was totally disgusted. "If she spent

more time getting that shop of hers together instead of running behind Lem, maybe she could pay back that loan I gave her."

Maxine stopped lacing the ham to stare her sister directly in the eye. "Teri, you are not hurting 'cause you gave Bird money for her shop." Maxine just hated when she brought up the money thing. So what that she and Miles were rich. She just wished Teri would get over it; everybody else had.

"*I* loaned her the money, Max," Teri reminded them, winding down her whipping. "As far as you're concerned, I'm an ATM—Automatically Teri's Money," she sassed.

"Now hush up," said Mother Joe, adding more pieces of chicken to the super-hot grease. "You two do this every Sunday."

Maxine cried, "Well she always startin' up—"

"Max, you go on and start up those biscuits," she said, talking over her to shut her up. "And Teri, you stop runnin' your family down."

Even Mother Joe didn't want to hear any more about Teri's money. "You need to pay more attention to your own man. You're already on husband number two," she told Teri, and then laughed at her own forwardness.

Teri was so shocked at being dissed by her mama that all she could do was whip those sweet potatoes to oblivion.

The upstairs bathroom in Mother Joe's house was just barely big enough for one. But for the moment, it was a secret love nest for Lem and Bird. Bird was propped up on the sink, and Lem was comfortably propped inside of her as they went for it with everybody downstairs waiting on Sunday dinner.

Lem was a real romantic. He loved to do it in out-of-the-way places, especially places where he had no business taking care of such business. He seemed to like it better when he had to be quick and sneaky. In his mind, there was no trade-off for that type of intensity.

Bird loved him to pieces. Nobody could make her feel as good as he did—nobody. What she loved the most was his dark Hershey-chocolate skin that glistened every time they made love. She loved to watch the sweat bead up on his bald head and the furrows made in it as he reached his climax. And Lem was the climax king!

For somebody who loved to be sneaky about his sex, he had a bad habit of screaming

at the top of his lungs right when he was coming. Today, Bird tried to keep him quiet by
covering his mouth with her hand. What with
the whole family right downstairs, she didn't
need to get caught like this. She didn't care if
he was her husband. When her hand could no
longer conceal his squeals, she stuffed her
panties in his mouth.

Teri stopped pouring the sweet potato
mixture into the pie shells and wondered
about the sound she heard. Maxine was
rolling out biscuits and Mother Joe was
turning her chicken. No one else seemed to
notice, so she shrugged it off and smoothed
the top of the pies in preparation for the
oven.

The kitchen door swung open and
Ahmad came in to watch the ladies work.

"Hey baby," Maxine called to him
sweetly.

He'd been around this cooking scenario
long enough to know how to do a few
things himself. After assessing who was
doing what, it was the biscuits he decided
he wanted to help with.

"Ooh mama, you making biscuits?" he
asked his mother.

"Uh-huh," she answered, continuing to press them out using a glass as a cutter.

"I wanna make some."

"Sure baby," she said, passing him the glass. "Now press hard like I taught you."

Ahmad took the glass and pushed down in the dough, making perfectly round biscuits. Maxine looked at him lovingly. She couldn't help thinking that he was her miracle baby. Every time he was near her, tears came to her eyes.

Teri stared at the mother and son exchange. Her expression was mixed with jealousy and resentment. She was jealous of the relationship Ahmad and Maxine shared, and she knew that Maxine had done a superior job in raising her nephew to be a fine young man. But she and Miles had waited to try, and were now having trouble making a baby. She was also resentful because she chose professional success over having a family. It was not that she could not have children. But she and Miles had waited to try, and were now having trouble making a baby. She had been pregnant twice, once in her first marriage and once with Miles. Both times ended in abortion; both times her decision and without either husband's knowledge. As she witnessed this exchange now, she was not so sure that she had done the right thing. Sure, she was successful, but at what price.

"All right, all right," Maxine told Ahmad after he did several biscuits, "that's enough. Now go on over there and wash your hands before you get your clothes dirty."

Washing his hands at the sink, he took a whiff of the aroma from the stove. "Big Mama, that chicken smells good. I can't wait to get me a piece of that," he told her. He went to her side, absentmindedly tossing the dish towel he dried his hands with onto the stove.

Mother Joe snatched up the towel quickly and grabbed up his cheeks in her hand. "Ooh baby, don't ever put anything like this on the stove. You'll burn the house down," she said almost in a whisper.

"Yes, ma'am," he said, understanding her clearly.

"Remember that time Bird almost burned the house down?" Teri laughed.

"Yeah, but that girl can sure burn some hair now," Maxine defended.

Ahmad began eating right out of the can of pineapples that Maxine was using to dress the ham. His eyes dropped to Mother Joe's leg. He wanted her good-tasting fried chicken, but not at the expense of her legs getting so swollen, bruised, and green. Two of her toes had already been amputated. He didn't want to lose anymore of his Big Mama to surgery. He was just about to suggest that she sit down, when he noticed she had caught fire.

His little eyes jumped clean out of his head. "Big Mama! Your arm!"

"Mama!" Maxine screamed, leading her to the sink and turning on the cold water.

"Get me some butter," cried Mother Joe.

"You don't need butter, you need ice," shouted Teri, running to the freezer.

Maxine asked, "Mama, you ain't been taking your insulin, have you?" Mother Joe jerked her arm away and turned her back to Maxine's inquisition. "And I bet you ain't been to the doctor, either."

Teri placed an ice pack on the arm. Mother Joe was riled up now about Maxine's questions. "Maxine, I told you I don't need no doctor. There ain't nothing my herbs, a little salve, and my turpentine won't cure."

An old Mississippi myth was that turpentine was good for an open wound. It was believed to be a germ killer, used like peroxide. Old people thought that it took out infection and that the more it burned, the more it healed. Mother Joe was a believer of this myth and used the paint remover on her wounds in conjunction with her salves that she made from herbs in the garden.

Maxine didn't care what the old folks thought. She was fed up. She did not want to see her mother die due to stubbornness and some myth that was not applicable in the advanced stages of her disease. "All of those concoctions from back in the day may be able to cure some things. Except your diabetes," Maxine said definitively and convincingly.

Mother Joe knew she could no longer belabor this point. All she could do was sigh.

The duty of blessing the food belonged exclusively to Reverend Williams. It was the one way for him to earn his permanent seat at the Joseph dinner table. The Reverend had a decent enough congregation—respectable, in fact. The Antioch Baptist Church roster boasted over 2,000 members and was a landmark in the community. Reverend Williams's father had founded the church in the early 1950s upon his arrival in Chicago from Mississippi. The Joseph's and the Williams's both had that Mississippi-to-Chicago connection.

Mother Joe, Grandfather Joseph, and Reverend Williams had been friends long before their migration to the north. They had been neighbors all of their lives. Mother Joe married the boy from down the street, and Reverend Williams married one of her fourth cousins. So that made him family—if you cared to count cousins that far removed.

Grandfather Joe and the Reverend even bought a little storefront together and started a social organization called "The Greenville, Mississippi, Club." It was a gathering place for folks from their hometown and state to come and enjoy good music and good food and to keep the memory of their Southern roots alive.

This Sunday afternoon, the Reverend was holding his hands in the air in prayer. "Bless this bread, bless this meat, bless my stomach, 'cause I'm gon' eat."

"Amen, Reverend," everyone chimed in, shaking their heads at his blatant greed while he grabbed the biggest chicken leg on the platter.

Mother Joe loved this day of gathering. At the dinner table, the family could engage in conversations about their work, what went on during their week, and even their dreams. "I dreamed about fishes last night," she teasingly informed her clan. A chorus of denials sang from each of the girls. Maxine pointed her fingers at her sisters.

Lem was perplexed. "What does that mean. Fishes?"

"It means that some family member is coming," explained Bird, "or they're pregnant."

"Or gonna get pregnant," Maxine said, rubbing her nine-month rounded belly. "That's right, because this is the last fish dream right here," she confirmed, indicating that Mother Joe's dreams were usually correct. The last time she had had a fish dream, Maxine turned up pregnant.

Teri and Miles exchanged a look. The pregnant thing was a huge bone of contention between them.

Miles suddenly remembered a part of another saying, "Never sweep the dust straight out the door . . ."

Kenny filled in the rest, "If you do, you will sweep out the good fortunes with it."

"Yeah right, whatever that means," Miles confessed, laughing.

These were some of the superstitions

that had always peppered Grandfather Joseph's conversations. Mississippi myths— they were part of his roots, and he was full of them. As if on cue, everyone at the table reflected a moment on their loved one who was no longer among them.

"Our daddy was the most superstitious man you could have ever met," Bird said, filling Lem in on this piece of their lives.

Trying hard to fit into the family conversation while they were on the topic of superstitions, Lem announced, "Hey, I have something." Everyone turned their attention toward him. "Don't split the pole and don't step on a crack or you'll break your mama's back," he finished. He was the only one laughing at his own joke.

Bird felt sorry for Lem, because she knew what he was trying to do. It was important to both of them that the family accepted Lem. She broke the silence by looking around at everyone's plates and offering up the item she made for dinner, "How are my fish cakes?"

The answer was evident, for the fish cakes were still piled on the platter untouched. Not one to allow his new bride to feel slighted, Lem took it upon himself to eat more than his fair share of the patties. "It's good," he said, chomping on a mouthful.

"I'll try them later," stated Miles gently.

Maxine came to her baby sister's rescue, "Aw Bird, you don't have to worry about cooking, because you know you can do some hair. And we all know Miss Teri can't cook a thing. That's why Mama made me cook all the time," she stated, fully intending for it to be an insult. "Ain't that right, Ma?"

"I wasn't in the kitchen like you, because Mama and Daddy kept my head in the books," Teri sarcastically refuted. "That's why *I'm* a successful lawyer."

"And that's why *I'm* a successful wife and mother," Maxine dug back.

"Girl, I don't even know why you're lying about me not being able to cook."

"Because you can't, and we all know that."

"We all know that I make the cornbread every week."

"I hardly call adding water to Jiffy making cornbread," Maxine said, rolling her eyes.

"Stop lying, Max, you know I make cornbread from scratch, and I have been since before you were born."

"Okay then, cornbread. What's in making cornbread?" Maxine continued. "Is that cooking?"

"Well, guess what, I can afford to have my own chef if I want," Teri said, intending to silence Maxine. "How 'bout that?" she sang back childishly.

Maxine dropped her fork in disgust, "Now why you got to bring up the money thing. You always got to bring up money. This conversation is about cooking and not money."

Ahmad buried his face in his glass of Kool-Aid and thought about how his mom and Aunt Teri just couldn't seem to get along. He had heard that it all went sour between them years ago, way before he was born . . .

When the Joseph girls were just teens back in the late 1970s, it was a rule that if one of them had a date, she had to bring along another family member. Teri always took Maxine. One night, Teri's date turned out to be Kenny—Maxine's future husband. At the skating rink, Teri was busy leaning on Kenny for support as she learned how to keep herself up on the skates. Meanwhile, Maxine was zooming around the rink showing off. It was important to Teri that she learned how to master the activity— skating was a really in thing to do in Chicago.

Kenny was impressed with Maxine's skating ability, and right in the middle of her showing off, she fell near the struggling couple. Apparently, Kenny was impressed with more than just Maxine's skating ability, because it took him less than two seconds to leave Teri behind and race to Maxine's rescue. When he helped her up, something happened between them that they were even then unable to describe.

Teri, green with envy, witnessed this tender moment between her beau and her baby sister. She could not keep herself balanced. She fell down hard without anyone to come to her rescue.

The next day, Teri walked down her street and noticed Kenny's 1974 Cutlass Supreme across the street from her house. Elated that he had come by to see her, she bopped over to his car to find that all of the windows were fogged. As she got closer to the car, the pit of her stomach fell to the ground. He was with another girl.

Boldly, Teri knocked on the window of the car, determined to see who her boyfriend had the audacity to be making out with across the street from her very own house. As the hands inside wiped the fog from the windows, Teri saw that the girl in the car was Maxine, who was speechless. Kenny was guilty, and Teri was aghast.

Teri quickly recovered from her shock and pulled Maxine out of the car by her hair, snatching out handfuls. Maxine screamed in pain and gave Teri a he-man push in the face that sent her falling in the street, books and papers flying everywhere. Then the two sisters went nuts at each other, swinging, scratching, and crying at the same time.

Kenny could not believe that all of this carrying on was because of him. He was sorry that he liked Maxine more than Teri, but he never wanted it to end up this way— a public brawl in the streets, heavyweight-champion style. After being frozen in his seat as witness to the unfortunate scene, he got out of the car and tried to break them up. Teri punched him in the nose and stormed off to her house.

Ahmad sipped his Kool-Aid slowly, thinking about the story that he had heard from other

family members but never dared to ask his
mother about for confirmation. Looking at
the two of them argue now, even his ten-
year-old mind could reasonably figure that
the dissension between them started when
his mom took his dad right from under his
Aunt Teri's nose. Still, why couldn't they all
just get along?

Teri and Maxine continued to bicker
loudly before they were silenced by Mother
Joe. "Cut out all that mess!" If Mother Joe
was forced to speak up, then the situation
was getting totally out of hand. "I get tired
of this every week. All of that 'who shot
Johnny.' Shut up and eat your dinner."

Knowing that each of the sisters were
resentful of the other's lifestyle, Kenny tried
to break up the tension by asking, "So Lem,
why did you go to the joint?"

Maxine kicked Kenny under the table.
She knew what he was trying to do, but
wished he hadn't. As silence swept the
room, it was evident that the question was a
poor one.

Kenny quickly figured out that his wife
didn't like his choice of icebreakers.
"What?" he questioned after he was kicked.
"Well, we don't know all the facts," he rea-
soned, hoping it would excuse his behavior.

Around the table, everyone was embarrassed. Lem could see it. He had seen for himself how the Joseph family used Sunday dinner as the Inquisition. It was just a matter of time before he was challenged to fess up with his story. Now or never, he thought.

"Look, I ain't gon' lie," Lem began. "I made a mistake, a stupid mistake. I came here from New York to help my cousin out, and I guess I just got caught," he said, relieved.

"Doing?" Kenny questioned, not letting him get off the hook with such a measly, mousy explanation and no details.

The family did not share in his timing. As if in unison, they wailed at him, "Kenny!"

Seeing the family behind him, Lem got the courage to speak, "It's a'ight. I got caught sellin' a little somethin' somethin' an' . . ."

Bird interjected, taking up for her man, "And he's paid his debt to society. Okay," she stressed, hoping that they could drop it at this moment. "It's no different from daddy and his gambling."

She had Lem's attention now, "Really." Maybe starting this conversation about why he went to the joint wasn't so bad after all,

Lem thought. Look at the revelation that came from it. "So your pops rolled them dice—did a little number's thang?" the tone of his voice was actually in admiration, as if to say, "You go, Grandfather Joseph."

Bird looked at her mother's face and she was immediately sorry for airing that bit of dirty laundry.

"We sometimes make bad choices in life," Mother Joe said, taking a deep breath. "My husband's was gambling. And he was bad at it. In fact, we almost lost this house." The three girls who had been avoiding her eyes looked directly at her now. That house meant everything to their mother and them. At last, they saw how painful it was for Mother Joe to have this discussion, but she continued.

"But I worked on my hands and knees. Cleaned up after white folks, did ironin' and laundry. An' on top of that, took in my dead sister's child," she said, sighing deeply as if a movie camera flashed those scenes before her. Even though she had made it through, it was apparent the pain was still there.

"You do what you have to do to stay strong . . . to save family," she said seriously to Lem. "Even if you stumble tryin'." Her tone suddenly took on that of a Baptist preacher winding up his sermon, "Y'all just remember one thing. One finger pointin' blame can't make no impact," she said, pointing her index finger. "But five fingers balled up can make a mighty blow." She showed them her fist. Shaking it toward Lem, she said, "You be that fist, Lem. This whole family has to be that fist."

Lem nodded a thank-you and actually felt accepted. Bird smiled happily, squeezed his thigh, and winked at her mother for putting the stamp of approval on her husband in front of the family.

The tone of the Sunday gathering bounced back to its normal happy state. Mashed potatoes were passed, forks clanged, and hearty appetites were satisfied.

Suddenly, a foxy young woman stood in the doorway and silently witnessed the scene. For a moment, all she could do was stare, absorbing the gaiety before her. The aroma of the food. The lively conversation. Yes, she was home. "Hi, y'all," she said.

Everyone turned to see the twenty-one-year-old standing there, dressed in the ultimate fly-girl attire: leopard coat, dark shades, skin-tight bodysuit, high heels, and expertly applied makeup. Simply put, she was glamorous. The family was stunned to see her. Forks fell to plates, mouths flew open, and eyebrows inched toward hairlines as curious looks were exchanged.

Only Mother Joe jumped up to receive her. "Oh my God, Faith," she said warmly, giving her a comforting hug.

"Mother Joe!" Faith cried, resting in the comfort of her embrace. "Oh, how I've missed you."

Ahmad buried his face in the Kool-Aid glass again. He felt the glass was the safest way to cover the exhibition of his real emotions without getting caught by his mother. He knew, being only ten, that certain things were not supposed to register with him as items of importance. But for Cousin Faith to show up during Sunday dinner, Lord have mercy that meant big-time trouble.

Ahmad had constantly heard Big Mama whispering about her dead sister's child. Last they heard, she was working as a dancer at a strip bar in California. Then she was supposedly discovered by some guy who put her in a few music videos. Ahmad smiled at that. Wow, my cousin is famous, he thought, finally taking his Kool-Aid glass away from his face.

Bird whispered to Teri and Maxine over the table, "Why did she come back here?"

"I don't know," answered Teri furiously. "But I'm not letting her stay here with mama again. You remember what happened last time." They stared at each other, each with their own looks of disgust. Oh, yeah. They remembered.

Maxine spoke up first, "Well then, Teri is taking hoochie mama in." Teri began to protest, but Maxine continued, "She is not staying with me, Kenny, and the kids. Oh no!"

Mother Joe helped Ahmad out of his chair. "Ahmad, kiss your cousin Faith."

"Ooh, you are sooo big," she said, cuddling him inside of her huge leopard coat.

"And Reverend, this is my sister's child," said Mother Joe, making sure all introductions were complete.

In his ever mannish way, the Reverend reached for Faith around her exposed midriff and tried to tickle her as he gave her a hug. "Ooh, sweetie, you sure are pretty."

Faith jumped back and slapped his hand, laughing, "Reverend, stop that!"

Maxine decided to greet Faith, and just as she stood, she grabbed her stomach in pain.

"Oh Lord, she's in labor," Mother Joe said knowingly.

The bustling for preparations began. Kenny ran to get her coat. Teri stood with the phone in her hand. "Max, what's the number to your doctor?" she shouted, trying to be heard. "Kenny, anybody! What's the number to her doctor?"

4

At the Michael Reese Hospital's maternity ward later that evening, Kenny was still dressed in his green scrubs. As he held his new baby girl up to the glass for the family to see, everyone began cooing, waving, and talking baby talk at her. Except Teri.

She was actually numb with the emptiness of her womb. The longing for a child hurt her deep, just like Maxine's continued digs about being a good wife and mother. The intensity of her longing scared her. It shook her very being to the point of her needing to take a seat at the end of the hall, away from the commotion.

Ahmad noticed that Mother Joe wasn't at the window, either. He went searching and found her asleep in the waiting room. All of that commotion had exhausted her. He remembered a time when Mother Joe would have been the leader of the pack, jumping about at the family's good news. But as Ahmad looked at her bandaged hand in her lap, he saw that her coloring was all wrong. As happy as he had been a moment ago, now he was equally sad.

The office of Dr. Benson was no different from any other, with its eerie quietness and an odor that reeked of antiseptic. The anxiety was extremely high among the Joseph girls, because they had been summoned for this meeting with Dr. Benson following Mother Joe's checkup.

The silence in the room was stifling. Mother Joe stared out into space from where she sat on the examination table. Her daughters were spread around her. Everyone was in a somber mood about her health and the necessary surgery to be scheduled. Mother Joe refused to accept the diagnosis and tuned out the world.

"Try to convince her," Dr. Benson said, stressing the urgency before exiting the room. "It's important."

Mother Joe grunted behind him as he closed the door, "I'm not getting my leg cut off!"

Teri stared at her mother in disbelief. "You have to!" she shouted, beginning to get too emotional. Calm down, she thought, before speaking. Try another approach . . . reason. Yeah that's it, reason. "No blood is flowing to your leg. You're a diabetic. You don't keep your sugar balanced and you don't watch what you eat." There, she thought, that was reasonable enough.

Maxine was not having reason play a part of the conversation. This was her mama they were talking about here. "And you don't take your medicine," she angrily accused. It was an accurate accusation. Mother Joe did not take her medicine, and it was no secret at all. The family members just hoped one day she would snap to her senses and begin following the doctor's orders.

Mother Joe felt that she would accept her fate, but neither doctors nor daughters would dictate what was best for her to do about her health. "Nobody's gonna cut my leg off!" she shouted sternly to them, looking each one in the face very seriously. "And that is FINAL!"

Bird touched Maxine and Teri, encouraging them to calm down. The room reverberated with silence. The sisters sighed heavily. Clearly, their mother knew the ramifications of delaying this surgery. Tears formed in their eyes as they came to realize that their beloved mother was preparing to meet her maker. Mother Joe was distraught, because as she looked into each of her children's faces, she realized that they knew she was ready to die. She had raised them well. She thought that now, after she was gone, the test of just how well they were nurtured would be evident.

Everyone who knew Mother Joe knew that she was a mother to all. Nothing was more precious to her than her children, though. People outside of the family envied the love and care that she displayed for the girls, and many wished they, too, were a part of her family. She would always tell them, "Mama won't always be around to tell you what to do. Some thangs you're gonna have to figure out for yourselves, and I've taught you enough to do that."

There was an old saying: "A mother's work is never done." Well, as a saddened Mother Joe looked around the room at Maxine, Teri, and Bird, she could not help but think, Yes, my work is done. And even though she was not smiling on the outside, the thought brought a smile to her heart.

The huge sign outside of the building read "Bird's Beauty Salon." There were balloons and ribbons and another sign that proudly announced "Opening Day." It was a happy day for Bird. Although she had been open for business for a couple of months, she had been working hard toward this official grand opening. And it was a success.

The salon was packed with women of all ages. Lively gossip filled the air with the regular beauty-shop banter. Bird and her staff were blessedly busy. Jada, the heavy-set manicurist, was full of the most accurate gossip that side of Chicago. Harome, the flamboyant male hairdresser, and Bird were running around doing several clients at once. Business was booming.

Ahmad worked there after school sweeping and dumping trash. He was glad to do anything he could to help his Aunt Bird. She was secretly his favorite auntie. So if he could be around her, earn a little money, and listen to all of the latest gossip, he was set.

All conversation ceased, however, when an immaculately dressed brother entered the salon. Ahmad recognized him instantly as the dude who was feeling all over Bird at her wedding. What did he want? Ahmad thought, pretending to sweep the floor.

Of course, there was nothing wrong with Simuel showing up at his ex-girlfriend's opening day to wish her well, but arriving dressed to a T in an Armani suit that looked as if it were sewed on him did raise some suspicion. He looked good and he knew it, so he posed in the doorway and allowed the women to get a real good look. His looks were reminiscent of the phrase, "You look so good you could be on the cover of *Ebony* magazine." Simuel was well over six feet and had ultra-smooth mocha colored skin, a thick black mustache over perfect pearly whites. Yes Lordy, Simuel St. James was all of that and a slice of sweet potato pie.

He strolled over to Bird and tried to kiss her on the lips, but she offered up her cheek in time. Ahmad was watching, armed with the broom, and he didn't like what he saw.

"Very nice," Simuel said, inspecting the

salon. "So Teri got off the dime and gave you money to open up your own shop, huh?"

Bird got annoyed. She did not appreciate him in the least sauntering his self into her shop and talking about how her accomplishment was made. "She didn't *give* me anything. It was an investment," she informed him, wishing that he'd just say congratulations and scram.

"See, if you'da come to me, I'd've given it to you," he let her know suggestively.

"Oh yeah," Bird replied, sick of his little innuendoes, "at what cost?" She moved around to the other side of the client whose head was caught in the middle of their banter. And girlfriend sat there not annoyed in the least; actually, she clearly enjoyed the exchange. Her eyes moved back and forth like she was watching a tennis match.

Simuel smiled. "How much are you willing to sacrifice?" he asked.

Continuing her work, Bird did not give him the satisfaction of answering such a foolish question. He took her silence as an opportunity to look at her behind and stroked his chin for optimum inspection.

"Girl, you are getting *thick*! You know, you always was the finest of all your sisters," he commented, enjoying his view.

"Please," she responded, wanting him to understand that his flattery was not going to reap him a single benefit. "When I was young, my daddy always said I was the ugliest."

"Well, you must have been the ugliest to come out this fine," Simuel said, throwing out all of his best lines.

Ahmad couldn't hear too well from where he was working, so he swept his way toward them. As he got close enough to see and hear, Simuel reached into his pocket and pulled out a small box. He handed it to her, but Bird stopped working and took a step back from him.

"I'm married, okay. Whatever we had was over. Forget about it," she announced furiously. "'Sides, my husband's name is written all over my kitty kat."

"Uh-huh," he said, simulating a laugh and placing the gift in Bird's hand anyway. "I know you like the finer things in life." He watched her hesitantly open the box and knew she was trying to contain that she was impressed. He knew her well enough to recognize that sparkle in her eye when she was pleased.

"And I know your man can't afford to buy shit like this for you," he said, digging himself further into a hole. "Him just getting out of jail and all."

Bird's smile disappeared and she snapped the box shut. Simuel knew she was affected, and he stroked the side of her face seductively. "When you need me . . . call me." Then he spun around on his heels and took an I-know-I-look-good exit stride to the front door as easily as he had entered.

Everyone in the shop was watching Bird, who was flustered and totally overwhelmed by her gift. She looked into Ahmad's face and saw him trying to process what he had seen.

"Come here, Harome," she summoned. She handed him the gift.

When he opened the box, he screamed and pretended to faint. Everyone rushed over to see the gorgeous and very expensive diamond bracelet. "Miss Thing," Harome raved, fanning himself as he lifted the bracelet to put it around his wrist, "I *must* borrow this."

Bird gave him a help-yourself wave of her hand and went back to work.

THE LARGE, LUXURIOUS DUPLEX CONDOMINIUM owned by Miles and Teri on Chicago's lakefront was beautifully furnished, and they were proud of it. Miles had put his culinary skills to use on an Italian dinner. Spaghetti, his specialty, garlic bread, and a salad were waiting in the kitchen. He and Ahmad were setting the kitchen table with candles.

Miles loved cooking and making their home lovely for the arrival of his wife. He made it a priority to be home every evening waiting for her. Teri worked too hard. Not that Miles did not, but he believed in the hierarchy of keeping family first and career second. In his opinion, being a success did not mean working twelve to thirteen hours a day. He felt that he would be even more respected in his profession if he proved that he could get all of his work accomplished during regular business hours. A late night here and there—sure, everybody put those in occasionally—but every night, no sir, not Miles. Besides, he wanted to do something else with his life when he grew up.

The law thing was just the means to meet his musical dream. While his days were taken up with work, his evenings were filled with music, and, if she would allow, a little romance with his wife. Usually, he would write lyrics or practice a song or two before Teri came home, so she would not be annoyed with his craft. By the time she arrived, she would generally be too exhausted to do anything other than eat, shower, and get into bed. And even after working extremely long hours, she would still get into bed with some work to read for the next day. Their relationship suffered. Miles was adamant, though, that by being the constant in her life, their marriage would be sustained. And the passion he put into his music was the evidence of his true feelings.

Teri blew in late, in her business suit and with briefcase in hand. She was pleasantly surprised to see her nephew. "Hi sweetie," she said, and she went to Ahmad to plant a kiss on his head. "You staying with us?" Ahmad nodded yes.

"Kenny and Max need a night off," Miles volunteered. "Kelly's staying with Bird."

Teri was exhausted. All she could do was kick off her shoes. She didn't need an excuse for Ahmad to visit. He even had his own room. It had been a long time, though, since Teri and Ahmad had done anything together. She must make some time for him, she thought. She had to figure out a way to let him know how important he was in her life.

She sat long enough to inhale the aroma of the garlic wafting in the air. Good, she thought, I'm starving. Thank God for Miles and his cooking; otherwise, she would starve.

Ahmad saw his Aunt relaxing after a hard day, and while he didn't want to interrupt her ritual of trying to unwind, he needed to pose a very important question that had been on his mind. "Aunt Teri, is Big Mama really gonna get her leg cut off?"

She stroked his head, knowing he was concerned. "You're worried, aren't you?"

Ahmad nodded, but no one could ever know just how concerned he was. He was afraid to really let everybody know, because he didn't want them to see him cry. If he started crying, everyone would start crying. It would be one big cryfest over something that would probably turn out okay.

Miles took a long, serious look at his wife and sensed her longing for a child. He put a plate in front of her, lit the candles, and diverted the conversation away from his suspicions. "Looks like that case is kicking your butt."

Teri agreed. "And the jury may be out I don't know how long," she reported, taking off her jacket and pulling her blouse out of her skirt. "Plus, the firm is pushing hard for me to make partner."

"But that's what you want, right? To make partner," Miles said it in a "why-are-you-surprised-I-thought-that's-what-you-wanted" tone.

Teri glared at Miles. She did not like his dig, but she needed to be careful not to express too much with Ahmad present. "All attorneys worth their salt want to make partner, Miles." She knew this was not a goal of his, and the insult was intentional. "Are you gonna run it down to me now . . . again . . . what you think I should be doing at my job?"

Ahmad thought, Oh boy, here we go. Another fight. She had irked Miles now, and he stopped eating and lit a cigarette, just staring at her. The doorbell rang. Saved by the bell! Ahmad thought as he jumped up to get the door.

Teri immediately turned to Miles. "There's some money missing from our savings," she informed him, deliberately advising him that she kept track of the money. "Last week, there was $90,342, now it's—"

"I took $5,000 out," Miles said, interrupting her. "I used it for a down payment on studio time. Me and the fellas are going to record a CD," he said happily.

Teri's tone was not so happy, "A CD? Miles please." She chuckled sarcastically. "I thought you playing with that band was just a hobby. Who's gonna buy your CD?"

Miles dropped his fork in disgust. "Why would you say something like that?" he flared.

She began her explanation in her "world-according-to-Teri" fashion, "Miles, you're an attorney at a great firm with a great reputation. You could be making twice as much money if you spent more time on your job and skipped this music crap."

He did not even want to get started with her making reference to his music as crap. "I don't want to argue with you, counselor."

"Don't call me counselor!" she shouted.

"If I want to take $5,000 of my money out of the bank, I'll do it."

"Only $31,132 is your money," she informed him.

Miles was beyond disgust to learn that she was keeping such a well-balanced tick sheet of his and her money tallies. "Tomorrow, we're getting separate accounts!" he shouted, standing to leave.

"No. Wait!" Teri pleaded softening a bit. "Just for the book's sake, let me know when you write checks. Okay?"

"Fine," Miles conceded, but inside he was seething. He walked away from the table just as Faith and Ahmad came in the kitchen.

"Hey," said Faith, all light and lively— totally unaware of the war zone she had just

entered. "Thanks for lettin' me stay here."
She looked around at the condo, impressed.
"Your place is really fantastic. So where do I
put my stuff?"

Maxine was breast-feeding her beautiful
baby girl in the kitchen, wearing a lovely
negligee and matching robe. For the
moment, she enjoyed the solitude. The
baby was almost asleep and the other two
were with their aunties. Whew. It was a
good thing that she knew how to handle
the newborn-baby thing. Tonight, she
wanted to enjoy a bit of piece and quiet and
her wonderful husband.

Kenny came in the back door with a
huge box. "You gonna love this, for the
baby," he said, happily opening up the box.

Maxine was shocked at the laptop com-
puter.

Kenny was happier than a kid at
Christmas. "Check it out, this is for the
baby. A top-of-the-line Apple Performa. It's
got your color monitor, CD-ROM,
Internet, fax, e-mail."

His wife looked at him like he had gone
crazy. "I think she might be a little young
for that." Maxine had to smile as she put

the baby in the crib and covered her exposed breast.

Kenny stopped and watched her.

"What?" Maxine questioned knowingly.

"You look beautiful," Kenny complimented, thinking that after three kids, she looked the same to him as she did when he first fell in love with her. "You know what . . . wait right there."

Suddenly, the lights dimmed and the speakers blasted Marvin Gaye's "Sexual Healing." Kenny returned to the room with a sheepish grin on his face.

"Man, what are you up to?" Maxine asked as she was swept into his arms for a slow grind. As they danced, Kenny began kissing her ears, shoulders, and neck. As they kissed, he began feeling her butt with loving desire.

"Now you know you gotta wait six weeks," Maxine reminded him. Kenny looked over at the calendar where he had circled this date, which indeed marked six weeks. They had been through this twice before, and he knew the drill. Maxine smiled at her husband's consideration and touched his face lovingly. They kissed again and pretended not to hear a knock at the door.

Kenny asked unbelievingly, "You hear that?"

"There is somebody at the door," Maxine relinquished. They tried to keep kissing, but the knocking persisted.

Grunting while opening the door, Kenny saw Lem was the unexpected visitor. "Brotha-man, this had better be good. I was two seconds from . . ."

Lem felt terrible. "I don't even know why I'm here. I just . . . I . . ." He was so embarrassed at the interruption he caused that he threw up his hands and began to walk off.

Maxine pulled him back and gave him a kiss hello. Looking at the sleeping newborn in the crib, Lem's thoughts were swimming around his head so fast that he still could not get himself together.

"Man, I just need to talk to you a moment," he told Kenny. "It's kinda personal."

Picking up the baby, Maxine went to Kenny and whispered in his ear, trying to be as understanding as always. Kenny grinned a wide smile at the sweetness she spoke and patted her on the butt as she left.

"So what's up?" Kenny said to Lem.

He honestly didn't know where to start.

Finally, he spit it out. "I got fired from my job today. I, uh, lied on my application. They ask if you ever been convicted. I checked no," he said in one breath.

Kenny looked into Lem's eyes and saw that this confession was killing him.

Lem continued, "You and Miles got yourselves together on the job tip. I was just hopin' if you know anybody or if there was any job openings . . . I-I'll do anything."

Kenny knew that the pressure was on Lem to be a good provider for Bird. Teri had her own money, but Miles had just as much. Maxine did not have to work. Kenny was the owner of the towing company that had been in their family for three decades.

"I'm always looking for drivers down at the garage," Kenny told him.

Lem was proud and thankful. "I'm just lookin' for a hand, not a handout." Lem wanted to be clear about the issue. "You understand."

Kenny clearly understood. A man had to be a man, and he appreciated Lem's understanding of that. "We'll find you something," he promised, patting his back.

It felt as if a huge burden had been lifted off Lem's shoulders. Finding another job was the weight he was carrying on one side.

On the other side was another burden. "Thing is," he said, worried, "I gotta find a way to explain this to Bird."

"What?" Kenny asked.

"She's high maintenance, you know. She walks around the house in Chanel sandals an' shit, an' I don't wanna come off like I'm livin' off her."

Now Kenny understood what Lem was saying. "No, no, no. Don't tell her" was his advice.

"Why not?" Lem asked, not seeing the logic in another lie. It was a lie that brought him to Kenny's doorstep in the first place, interrupting the intimate evening with his wife.

Kenny saw that he had a little schooling to do for the young brother. "Listen, you don't want to tell a woman—"

"A black woman," Lem said, catching on now.

"*Especially* a black woman you ain't got a job," he explained. "It's all right for them to sit around the house, but let a man—"

"A brotha."

"Especially a brotha," Kenny stressed. "You might be fixing caps under the kitchen sink—"

"Watering the plants—"

"Washing the dishes . . . or taking the garbage out . . ." Kenny knew his message was clear now. Reaching into his pocket, he pulled out a few bills and handed the money to Lem. "Here is a little something. Remember, no matter what you do around the house, they will still consider you a—"

"Trifling nigga," said Lem. They both paused a moment, thinking about the wages women had placed on their heads.

"Don't tell her," they said at the same time.

Lem sat on the porch steps at Mother Joe's house and had a cigarette by himself in the dark. He was deep in thought about the conversation he had with Kenny earlier that evening. Initially, Kenny had successfully talked him into not telling Bird about getting fired from the job, but lying to his woman—his wife—Lem was not so sure that was a good decision. Allowing his head to fall back onto the banister, the depression he felt about the decision engulfed him.

Bird came up the walk with groceries and smiled when she saw her man outside. The closer she got, though, the more she could see that Lem's face was troubled. Her smile faded quickly.

"What's up. Why you sittin' outside?" she said, sitting on his lap and giving him a light kiss.

"I'm just thinking," Lem said, faking a smile and shrugging off her advances. "Not right now.

"Not right now," Bird repeated incredulously to herself. Wait, this could not be her hot-to-trot husband ready and willing to do it *any*where and *any*time telling her "not right now." Something was up.

"What's wrong with you?" she rightfully wanted to know.

"Nothin'," Lem repeated. He felt guilty as hell lying to her. What he was really thinking was that he needed to do a better job at his lying. "I'm just thinkin' 'bout stuff."

Good, Bird thought, he's opening up to me. She took what he said and flipped it to a sexual innuendo. "What kind of stuff?"

"Just stuff, a'ight. I've got a lot of shit on my mind right now."

"Come on Lem, don't be like that. Talk to me," Bird said, puzzled. He had never been so stubborn before. Typically, she could get anything out of him. And if it was a really big secret, all she had to do was wiggle on him a little bit here or there and he would give it up like a dump truck.

"How do you think it makes me feel?" Lem said, getting worked up.

"How was work?" Bird asked.

"It's all right," he answered.

"C'mon. Help me with the groceries."

Lem sat in silence, staring into the darkness.

"Did something happen today?" Bird questioned. "What happened?"

"Baby?" she quizzed sweetly.

Finally, he turned to her with a sigh. He wanted to tell her, really he did. But his pride could not let him do it just then.

6

At Michael Reese Hospital, Mother Joe lay in a mobile hospital bed that was being wheeled off for surgery. Every adult member of the family had to have a "little talk" with her before she was finally convinced to do what was best for her health.

The nurse came to a halt in front of the waiting room where the Joseph family sat. The anesthesia was taking its toll on Mother Joe, but though groggy, she was determined to stop by the waiting room to see her family.

Ahmad watched as everyone hugged and kissed his Big Mama. He was hiding behind his father. He would do all of his well-wishing from right there, thank you. Maxine called him over to the bed, knowing he was afraid to see his grandma in such a condition.

Mother Joe bent Ahmad's head down and kissed him. "Don't worry, Sweet Pea, I'll be just fine. I need you to stay strong," she told him.

Ahmad felt better now. Big Mama had given him an order she needed for him to carry out, and there was no way he would let her down.

Mother Joe motioned for Maxine to bend down to her lips so she could whisper orders for her. "You can't be defensive all the time with a chip on your shoulder," she began. "Your daddy always said you were the strongest, Maxine. The family's gonna need your strength now."

Though Maxine did not understand fully what she was saying, she acknowledged she understood anyway. It was time to leave, and the nurse wheeled Mother Joe down the long corridor. Teri and Bird fought back tears. Ahmad walked as far as he could behind the bed until it disappeared into the double doors at the end of the white hall-way.

For hours, everyone paced the waiting room's floor impatiently. Ahmad watched the entire family wait helplessly for the results of the surgery. There were occasional glances and inspirational touches, sighs of exasperation, silent prayers, and cold coffee sipped. It was killing them and he knew it.

As if right on cue, Ahmad saw Dr. Benson hastily make his way down the hospital corridor to the waiting room. At first, he smiled, but then Ahmad saw the look of concern on his face and knew that something was wrong. Panic swept the family as they met the doctor halfway down the hall.

They surrounded him. "I'm sorry. There was a problem. Your mother suffered a massive stroke during surgery and went into a diabetic coma."

Gasps of shock spread around the circle as they reluctantly followed Dr. Benson to the intensive care unit. Everyone went in except Ahmad. He stayed outside trying to collect his thoughts. A myriad of conversations he had had with Big Mama flooded his brain. The most recent conversation was as fresh as ever, *"Don't worry, Sweet Pea, I'll be just fine. I need you to stay strong."* With that in mind, though scared to death, Ahmad took a deep breath and entered the ICU.

Family members were spread throughout the room, surrounding Mother Joe's bed. When Ahmad entered, they turned to face him. He saw his family consoling one another. Beyond their concerned faces, he glimpsed Mother Joe lying on her bed, unconscious and hooked up to a variety of lifesaving machines. Kenny was covering Mother Joe's bandaged leg, so he didn't catch a peek.

Tears flowed in buckets down the boy's face as he cried for Big Mama. Maxine walked over to hug her son and tried to lead him back to the corridor, but he refused to leave. Remembering that it was Big Mama who taught little Ahmad to walk, his aunts and uncles could only guess at how much he knew he was losing.

Miles needed to get away from all of the crying for a while. Outside the hospital, he lit a cigarette to collect himself when he saw Teri standing by herself sobbing. They had argued constantly recently, but that did not erase his natural instinct to go to his wife.

He walked up behind Teri and reached

to console her. She was so distraught that her head just fell back onto his shoulders and the tears flowed. She was crying mostly for her mother, but she also wept for what her stubbornness had inflicted on her marriage. She did not have to be so difficult, and she knew it. It was a pitiful shame that it took such a tragedy for her to realize how much she loved her husband. It had been far too long since the two had physically come so close together.

Miles held her for a while and let her cry. He was concerned for her pain, but he knew that some of those tears were for their broken relationship as well. He didn't know what else to do other than stand there. So that's all he did. Somehow, they both knew that for the moment, it was going to have to be enough.

Ahmad sat in room 226 alone at the side of his grandma's bed. She was still in the coma, they said, but he chose to view it as her being asleep. Big Mama had been through a lot in her life. She needed to sleep. She was still breathing, wasn't she? So that meant that she would wake up soon, and he planned to be there when she did.

The medical equipment hooked up to Mother Joe was quietly humming. Ahmad looked down at her weak, ravaged body another moment and took her hand. He knew she would wake up soon. He just knew it.

What would we do without Mother Joe? he thought. He might as well get prepared for when that day came, because even if she made it through this episode, Ahmad knew that he would probably live to see the day Mother Joe died. His own selfishness set in. He just didn't want it to be now. Ahmad knew that without Big Mama, his family would fall apart.

He sat and waited.

7

LEM WAS SEATED IN THE PERSONNEL department office of a small commercial printing company. He was sweating buckets over the job application. Decked in his best suit and tie, he heard the roar of the printing machines in the background. Lem made sure everything was just right.

Then he stopped at the question: "Have you ever been convicted of a felony?" Lem hesitated. That lying thing didn't work out so well for him the last time. Should he lie again or tell the truth? He checked a box and took his finished application to the white man seated behind the desk.

The man adjusted his glasses and casually looked over the application. Lem studied each and every one of his expressions. The man finally got to the question checked "yes." This hit the man like a ton of bricks.

Taking off his glasses, he uncomfortably put down the application. "We'll call you," he said with a stern face.

Lem was frustrated. "But the sign outside your door says you're willing to train. Well, I got experience on presses—and I'm a quick learner! I can do the work."

"Like I said, we'll call you," the man repeated. He walked away leaving Lem numb.

The school bell rang and kids poured out onto the street running in every direction. Ahmad and two of his friends dressed warmly for the chilly weather, donned their backpacks, and started the walk home.

They laughed and played along their route, which took them under the train tracks of the El. A continuous horn got the kids attention, and Ahmad saw it was his

Uncle Lem behind the wheel of the Bronco. He pounded fists with his buddies and ran to get in the truck, which was blasting Jean Carne's "Don't Let It Go to Your Head" from one of the city's dusty radio stations.

"Why you all G'd up today, Uncle Lem," Ahmad asked, because Lem was still dressed in the interview suit he called a uniform.

"If I tell you somethin', promise you won't tell your mama or your nosy-ass aunties?"

Of course, Ahmad wanted to be down with his Uncle, so he nodded yes.

Lem felt he could trust Ahmad and that it would be all right to share his secret with him. "I was fired from my job last week. I been trying to find another one. 'Cept things ain't goin' so well," he admitted.

Ahmad wanted to properly process what he had heard. "Don't sweat it. You'll find a gig soon," he told his Uncle with total trust.

Lem had to smile at his attitude. "Think so, huh? You got a lotta confidence to be just a shorty."

"I get it from Big Mama, they say," Ahmad told him.

Lem laughed easily as he maneuvered through the afternoon traffic. "Here," Lem said, handing Ahmad his gloves. "Put these in the glove compartment.

Ahmad opened the glove compartment and immediately noticed the 9-millimeter Glock. Lem slammed its door shut and the smile disappeared.

He became serious with Ahmad. "You know I spent some time in prison, right?"

"Yeah. You was a big-time pharmaceuticals man."

Lem laughed at his choice of words and turned at an intersection. "Man, but I wouldn't've even been in jail if I'd been smart—like *you* seem to be."

Ahmad could see that Lem was trying to help him, but he didn't have a thing to worry about. Drugs and that other stuff were nowhere near the kinds of things that Ahmad had planned for himself. Besides, his mama would kill him.

"You know, Big Mama's always saying you gotta love yourself," the young boy advised, sounding more like a sixty-year-old. "Maybe you should try that. Just forget about what went down back then and step off to tomorrow."

Lem absorbed what the young man had so simply yet eloquently advised him to do. It took a ten-year-old to really tell him like it was. Out of the mouths of babes, he thought. Lem nodded that his words of wisdom had been received and would be upheld and respected. The two knocked fists in gentlemanly fashion.

Ahmad had taken up temporary residence at Miles's and Teri's condo while everyone was rotating duty at the hospital. So had Faith. She was blaring a boom box and teaching Ahmad the latest dance moves while performing her daily exercise ritual dressed in a revealing tank top and super-short shorts. She was an exquisite dancer. Faith transformed dance into an art form. Embracing and perfecting traditional steps, she made each movement her own. When she danced, her beauty was magnified.

Faith grabbed Miles by the hands and pulled him into the middle of the floor. He did not want to dance. He had not danced in ages, unless he counted dancing with his wife at Bird's wedding, which they did more out of obligation than desire. He couldn't remember when he and Teri had just gone out and had fun.

Ahmad and Faith chanted to egg him on, "Go Miles! Go Miles!"

Finally, he began to imitate Faith's version of the butterfly. They doubled over laughing at him.

As Teri approached the apartment, she heard all of the commotion inside and threw open the front door. She stopped in her tracks at the scene before her. Miles was totally embarrassed and stopped dancing. Teri looked discerningly at Faith's skimpy wardrobe, then at Ahmad and Miles, and stomped into the kitchen.

Miles followed her. "How is Mother Joe," he asked concerned.

"Not good. Now they're worried about infection," she said, exasperated. "On top of that, I won't be able to make it to your performance tonight," Teri said coolly, as if it didn't really matter. "I'm swamped with work, so . . ."

Treading this familiar territory once again, Miles was bothered by her aloofness. "You said that last week, and the week before that—"

"And next week, too, if I don't get my butt to the grindstone," she snapped, slamming her briefcase down on the counter. "So please, let's not argue about your music again, okay! Please!" she half pleaded and half demanded.

He closed his eyes and decided to tell her about a decision he had been considering, "I'm thinking about pursuing my music full-time."

"Have you lost your mind? Miles, you are not even that good!"

That was the final straw. "How much longer do you think I'm gonna take your insensitive condescending bullshit, Teri." He finally went off. "Now either you find the time for things I'm interested in or you can be by yourself!"

Faith and Ahmad had worked up a sweat dancing, and they entered the kitchen for a Kool-Aid refresher. It didn't require a law degree to detect the tension that lingered in the air. Miles was aghast at how determined Teri was to providing a zero support system for him, and he left the kitchen in disgust. Ahmad followed him.

Teri looked disapprovingly at Faith's workout gear. "Did you find a job yet?" If she had, that meant she would be out of her house sooner rather than later.

"No. It's hard to get motivated to look for a gig when I can't take labor seriously, you know?" Faith admitted. "I mean, the common man and woman spend hours of their lives achieving nothing but a paycheck."

She explained this all as if Teri actually cared, even though no one asked her. "And what does it do for the soul? Nothing," she concluded lightly.

Teri thought this girl was coo coo for Cocoa Puffs. "Well, I'm sure there's a lesson in there somewhere. That something so simple as *dancing* can take the place of hard work yet make everyone so joyful and content," she said trying, sarcastically, to step into her frame of reasoning for a moment.

Faith cracked up. "I don't like being here anymore than you want me here, Teri." She added more seriously, "I didn't ask to be 'between gigs.' And I thought I was staying at Mama Joe's ."

See, Teri thought, that "between gigs" shit was precisely the point that she was trying to talk to Miles about. Miles had responsibilities. He was to add to, not detract from, their financial stability.

Teri was not in the mood to play games. It was time she cut to the chase with her little cousin. "What are you doing back here, Faith? Weren't there enough men in L.A. just dying to rescue a scantily clad woman such as you."

Faith glared at Teri. She had never seen her get so real before. Teri's marriage was on the rocks, her workload had reached an unmanageable peak, and her mother was on the brink of death. It was clear even to Faith that Teri was not playing games. If you push a sister hard enough, as Teri had been pushed recently, the rugged South Side of Chicago attitude could jump out all over you. And even with all of Teri's sophistication, her Northwestern law degree, duplex condo on the lakefront, and $90,000 in the bank, unfortunately for Faith, she was about to feel that South Side thing run amuck all over her.

Teri stared Faith down. "Because the one thing you *won't* be doing this time," she said as she held up her fingers to tick off the things she would not tolerate like the family had in the past, "is running up Mama's credit, or making her cosign for a car and then leave her to pay the notes—"

"Why do you only remember the bad," Faith wailed.

Teri wasn't through with her yet. She only had up three fingers. There was more. "—Or get arrested and try to have Mama put up the house to post your bail, then skip town like you did in '93."

"I changed," Faith said softly.

Teri wanted to slap her face with the

open hand she had available after counting the scandalous activities from Faith's past. "Well, you read my lips, Miss 'I've changed,'" she snapped, hoping that she was making herself crystal damn clear, "you start any crap this time, and you'll find yourself on a bus back to LaLa so quick you won't have time to say bump and grind."

This was too much for Teri to deal with at one time. She needed to take three Tylenol and lay herself down somewhere before she killed somebody.

8

THE ENTIRE FAMILY WAS PRESENT AT the hospital, even though it was Saturday night and the head of their family remained comatose. They sat quietly around Mother Joe's bed while the machines that were hooked up all over her body kept up their beeping and buzzing.

Maxine broke the silence. "It's getting late and I still have to grocery shop for dinner tomorrow."

Everyone was somewhat surprised by the statement, but only Teri commented,

"Max, surely you don't expect to have a Sunday dinner tomorrow?"

Maxine was perplexed as to why Teri had asked such a question, but as she looked around the room, she saw that some agreed with Teri.

"Why not?" Maxine placed the question on the floor for anyone to refute.

Teri, the family counselor, jumped at the bait, "Jesus, Max! Mama's in a coma!" Teri and Maxine stared at one another.

Kenny tried to add his input, but Maxine cut him off. "I am not gonna let you ruin a forty-year family tradition."

Teri was on a roll with telling people how she felt, so she let Maxine have a taste. "What this is really about is my condo, me graduating from law school, and why you chose to get married at nineteen and drop out of college. No. This is about *your* jealousy, Max!"

Maxine was seriously taken aback, and as she was about to respond, Bird piped up, "Well, I say we vote."

Maxine replied, "Yeah. All those who don't want to have Sunday dinner tomorrow!" Maxine was quietly satisfied when no one raised their hand.

Now Maxine raised her hand and enthusiastically said to the group, "Hands in the air. All those who wanna be sitting in front of some chitlins, black-eyed peas, fried chicken, greens, and egg pie."

No one raised their hand. No one wanted to choose sides, not even Bird, who really did want the Sunday gathering. Maxine looked at Faith, who threw up her hands. Maxine then angrily looked to her husband, who quickly raised his hand.

"I won't let you disrespect Mama like she is already dead," Teri said as she gathered her things.

"You get on my fucking nerves," Maxine spit out in a blaze of fury, going after Teri's neck. Kenny held her back as the two began to argue over their mother's bed. Then everyone began arguing back and forth, throwing in their opinions and adding to the ever-increasing volume. All seemed oblivious to the woman who lay dying in their midst.

Ahmad and Kelly sat right outside the door listening as the adults argued about a stupid dinner. Not that the Sunday tradition was stupid, but for them to be carrying on while Mother Joe was lying there like that was terrible. The two kids could not help but cry, because they were glad that Big Mama could not see them this way.

Dr. Benson and a nurse rushed into the room amidst the arguing. "I'm sorry," he had to shout above them, "I'm going to have to ask all of you to leave, now! Mrs. Joseph needs quiet! Please. Go!"

Maxine and Kenny stormed out first and snatched Ahmad and Kelly from their chairs. Miles, Faith, Teri, and Lem followed.

Bird ran out last, calling after them, "Hey, wait. Come back you guys! *I'll* even cook tomorrow."

At high noon, Bird was in Mother Joe's kitchen sweating buckshots trying to prepare dinner alone. The kitchen was in disarray, with piles of food, supplies, and dishes scattered around. She tried to prepare oxtail stew, fried chicken, mustard greens, and peas without help from anyone. Being Bird's first time in the kitchen alone, she had out the recipe book, struggling with amounts of seasonings. She heard the church bells ring and wondered whether her family would show for dinner.

The table was set and the steaming hot food sat waiting to be consumed. The only guest who showed was Reverend Williams, chowing down as usual, as if he didn't even notice how unappetizing the meal looked. Never mind that, his plate was piled high as usual.

Lem could see that his wife was upset that no one else showed. It was the first time that the tradition of the Joseph family Sunday dinner had been broken.

Bird placed a tray of food for Uncle Pete in the usual spot on the floor in front of his bedroom door.

She knocked to announce, "Uncle Pete, dinner."

The cane quickly drew the food inside. A few moments later, he pushed out the tray and slammed his door in obvious disgust. Bird sighed heavily, vowing to spend more time working on her culinary skills.

Instead of allowing her disastrous Sunday dinner go to waste, Bird locked up the shop for lunch on Monday and invited Jada and Harome for leftovers. Bird opened the refrigerator to offer up the large quantity of food still available.

"So you cooked all this food and none of your people showed up?" Harome grilled.

"Girl, I know you wanted to slap some-body."

Jada grabbed a cold piece of chicken and found it rather tasty. "Well, we can help you get rid of some of this food—got to repre-sent," she said with her mouth full.

They heard a loud noise that alarmed everyone. "What was that?" Harome asked just as the noise occurred again.

Jada immediately grabbed a regular din-ner knife.

Harome laughed. "What are you gone do with that? Butter the burglar?"

Suddenly, the noise echoed again and the women armed themselves with brooms. Harome grabbed an umbrella.

It was Jada's turn to get him back, "And keep him dry?"

"Ssshh! Somebody's in here," said Bird. No one should have been home other than Uncle Pete, and he never came out of his room.

They all crept into the living room, sus-piciously looking around. The noise came from inside the bathroom's closed door. They inched toward the door and waited. When the door opened, all three were on the intruder's tail, attacking with brooms and the umbrella until the suspect fell to the floor yelling in pain. Harome dropped the umbrella, jumped on the intruder's back, and began to swing like a woman. Bird stopped swinging and noticed it was Lem wrapped in only a towel.

"Stop! Stop!" Bird screamed.

Harome stopped swinging and looked closely. "Boyfriend, ain't you s'posed to be at work?" he pointed out.

Lem was too frightened to speak as his towel fell to the ground displaying his naked body. All three mouths dropped open as Harome and the girls stared at Lem's manhood. Imported straight from the beaches of Jamaica, express-mailed to Chicago, the boy was hung.

Harome fanned himself and joked to Bird, "Girlfriend, you got it going on!"

Bird was pissed off now. She picked up the towel and tossed it to Lem so he could cover himself. She stormed into the bathroom and he followed close behind.

Harome whispered to Jada, "Did you see that thang?"

"I saw it . . . an' I don't believe it," she whispered back.

Bird was livid. She didn't even need to speak. The look on her face told Lem he had better have a good explanation as to why he was home taking a leisurely hot shower in the middle of a workday.

"I got fired," he said.

"What happened?" she questioned, gauging her words carefully because she was so pissed. "Can't take working a nine-to-five? You in trouble again?"

Lem hated this kind of confrontation. Now he wished he would have told her from the beginning, "No, no, they fired me 'cause they found out I lied on my application about being convicted."

"And you felt you couldn't tell me?" she asked, knowing this was painfully difficult for him.

"I wanted to tell you, but Kenny told me it would be in your best interest if you didn't know." He blurted this out, glad to be able to put that blame elsewhere.

"Kenny! You listened to Kenny?" she questioned in a "but-what-about-me-I'm-your-wife" tone. "What about us? What *we* have?"

Lem was hurt and embarrassed. "This ain't about us, it's about the system. It's bullshit!" he ranted. "They lock you up, then expect you to do somethin' better with your life. But when you get back out here, there ain't nothing, 'cause the crackers won't give you a second chance. So they don't leave you with nothin' but hustling again."

She reflected on the life of the Joseph family and their successes. Mother Joe had taught them to leave the excuses behind and to move ahead. "Lem, all that 'white-man shit' is old. I'm sick and tired of niggas using that as an excuse," she said.

"Look at me—look at our family—look at us" is what she wanted to scream. All around them were nothing but examples of how to overcome. She could not believe that Lem would not just open his eyes and see. It was laid out there before him.

"Hey," he said, aggravated, "I'm the one who's been on six fuckin' interviews! They won't hire me! So what the fuck do you know about being a *black man*!"

Bird cooled down a bit and sat on top of the toilet seat. She certainly did not want to have the "being a black man in America" conversation at the moment.

To avoid the argument, she said, "I . . . I'm sorry. You're right. I don't know what it's like to be a black man. Look, the shop is doing okay right now, so I can take care of any bills we have, okay? So don't let any of this discourage you. There are a bunch of people in the shop that might know of a job."

"I don't need your help, Bird. I can find my own job."

She was shocked and a little hurt by his comment, and she threw up her hands in a "whatever" gesture. At the same time, she kept glancing down between his legs.

Upset, Lem grabbed the towel defiantly and covered himself. "And stop looking at my dick!"

9

AHMAD SHOULD HAVE BEEN AT SCHOOL THE afternoon he entered the ICU to visit Mother Joe, but he needed to see her with nobody else around. He had not given up on the thought that she would wake up soon. Pulling up a chair, he took a look under the covers at the bandage where her leg had been. It felt impossible to control his emotions and stay strong with her in such a bad condition, but he was trying.

"I know you think I been avoiding you," he said out loud to her, convinced that she could hear him somehow, "but every time I come by to see you, there's always people around doin' stuff to you or arguing around you."

He was hoping that the confession of the family drama didn't stir her. She, like him, hated the arguing. She lay completely still.

"Anyway," he said, not knowing what else to say and not ready to leave either, "I . . . I know you're wondering how everyone else is doing."

It felt as good as ever for him to have a talk like this. Those were the best moments in his whole life—heart-to-heart conversations with Big Mama. She might not have responded back to him verbally, but Ahmad knew the ESP thing between them was still active and well.

So he decided to tell all, "Well, the family is not good. We didn't have Sunday dinner yesterday. Aunt Bird said nobody showed up." For Ahmad, that was a family emergency unto itself. What! No Sunday dinner. His stomach flip-flopped all night long at the thought of Mother Joe ever knowing such a betrayal had taken place.

He continued his conversation, "After church, Moms didn't feel like cooking at home, so daddy brought home some Micky D's. We were all on the toilet all night." He giggled at how good the McDonald's Big Mac and French fries tasted going down, but took its revenge on them later. It was a funny sight to describe after the fact, but not funny at all when a family of four each scrambled for bathrooms.

Ahmad exhaled loudly. "We need you, Big Mama," was his plea before he started to walk away. Then he turned around one last time. "Yeah . . . I was thinking that, too," he said to her as if responding to Mother Joe's question. "Maybe when you get out of here, I'll help you turn the ground over, as you call it, put some fertilizer down, get it ready for winter. Yeah, I'll help you," he told her reassuringly. He always helped her, and he wanted to make sure that she knew he was still the best helper she would ever have.

When he was about to leave, he stared at her and wanted to give her a kiss, but he was afraid to touch her with all of that stuff hooked up everywhere. Suddenly, he was compelled to touch her skin, and then he kissed her anyway. The familiar sensation made him smile even though she showed no outward response. Ahmad knew that her heart recognized his presence—and that was good enough for him.

Ahmad strolled casually down a busy street, swinging his backpack seemingly with not a care in the world. Seeing his grandma was just the pick-me-up his spirits were craving. A tow truck zoomed by at lightning speed, which caught his attention. He thought he saw a familiar face in the truck, and he became really scared . . . like he had seen a ghost. He kept looking down the street to make sure the truck was out of sight.

Releasing a sigh of relief, but not convinced he was safe from the big bad truck, Ahmad took off running and darted as fast as he could into an alley. It was a long industrial alley, but for the moment, it was Ahmad's personal Olympic track. He ran at top speed.

He was forced to slow down when he saw the same tow truck in the alley. The truck had shining chrome rims, bright lights, and a roaring engine. The words "Mad Dog" were printed on the truck in gold letters.

In complete shock, Ahmad watched the truck slowly make its approach toward him.

The engine was roaring, and Ahmad felt as if all his nerves were about to jump out of his skin. He was frozen in one spot. The truck kept coming until it stopped within inches of him.

The driver's door opened, and as he took off his shades, Ahmad looked like he had seen the devil. "Going somewhere?" Kenny asked his son.

Ahmad was speechless. All he could do was shake his head no.

Kenny hoisted him up to the passenger seat and revved the engine back onto the street.

As they drove, the father had a look of genuine concern, "So when are you gonna tell me why your butt is not in school?"

"I went to the hospital to see Big Mama," he said seriously while swallowing hard. "I had a dream last night that she came outta her coma . . . an' nobody was there with her. That's why I skipped school. I just wanted to see her by myself."

"I'm very proud of you, son," Kenny beamed.

"For what?"

"I know it's hard on you with your grandmom in the hospital. But you're handling it like a man."

"But I cried, though," the little man admitted.

"So! Men cry sometimes," said Kenny, even more proud of his son because he admitted he cried.

"I never seen you cry."

"Believe me, I've cried. I cried when the doctors told us you'd never walk," he said, squeezing Ahmad's shoulder. "You're strong son. Stronger than a lotta other folks in the family."

"I have to be," the little man insisted. "Big Mama wants me to be. If I'm not, she'll know."

Okay, the kid was bugging out now, Kenny thought. "How?" Kenny asked.

Ahmad did the *Twilight Zone* theme. "Do, do, do, do—Do, do, do, do. Remember?" His father might not realize the extent of the communication with his grandmother, but he knew his son believed what they had was extra-special. He was not about to dispute him. Ahmad saw a tape in the cassette player and popped it in.

Curiously, Kenny asked, "Ahmad, what you think your grandmom is thinking about right now?"

"She wants the family to stop fighting and have a Sunday dinner," he stated matter-of-factly.

Kenny chuckled and then had a thought. "Yo, youngblood, what say you and me hang out today?"

Ahmad grinned a smile of approval, "Yeah . . . Mad dog!"

A building with a large sign read KENNY TOWING COMPANY. The lot was packed with tow trucks and employees. Cars were being towed in and out of the lot as father and son entered the main building. Kenny spoke to his assistant, who was on the dispatch radio getting information and dictating it over the two-way radio. Completely tired and overworked, Kenny took a seat at his junk-covered desk.

He reflected on the day he had with his son and was happy that they had spent it together. Ahmad was still bouncy and fresh as if it were noon. "Youngblood, promise me something. A'ight? Don't tell your mama about today." He knew he should have taken Ahmad to school, but due to the circumstances, he just could not do it. "If she found out you hung out with me instead of being in school, she'd skin both of us alive. Like a squirrel. You ever seen a squirrel being skinned?" he asked.

Ahmad shook his head no.

"It's ugly. Ugly. Today is our little secret, okay?" Kenny concluded, sealing the manly bond between them.

"What'd we do today?" Ahmad asked, being wise.

They did their special fist knock to seal the pact tightly.

"You going to school tomorrow," Kenny commanded.

MILES WAS SEATED AT THE KEYBOARDS AS he and his eleven-piece band called Milestone jammed to a full-house capacity. He was playing in one of the city's most classy nightclubs. The patrons of Chick Rick's were all dressed to impress. Many of them had come especially to see Milestone perform.

Initially, Miles had arranged with the booking manager a one-night-only performance with no pay. The deal was sealed. If the manager liked them, then they would discuss a one night a week deal with pay; if he didn't, Milestone would come back when they were better. The booking manager was so impressed with the group and the audience's response that he had no choice but to book them for three nights a week.

Milestone consisted of five singers and six musicians including Miles. It was the band that he had dreamed about for years, and it took him almost six months to get the blend just right. During that time, he had run through almost every musician and singer in Chicago, adding a vocalist here, taking out a guitarist there. He had spent most of his free time under the guise of it being a hobby, scouring the clubs over the entire city and even attending talent shows until he found the sound that he felt was perfection.

Faith entered the smoky club with a male friend just as the band started to play. She began grooving to the music immediately and made her way to the front of the packed club so she could get a better view of Miles singing and playing at the keyboards.

She was impressed not only with the sound of the group, but also with their look. She could not help but think that Miles had purposely put together a group of ultra-fine men as an attention-getter. If that was not his intention, it was certainly an extra added plus, she mused, looking into each of the performers' faces.

The music was brilliantly composed, as were the lyrics. Faith always picked apart each aspect of music, and she did the same as she listened to the performance. The lyrics, she thought, were an ode to his and Teri's broken relationship:

> *Sometimes I feel so alone baby, I call you up but there's no one at home.*
>
> *Girl, I care about you. I'm there for you, so why don't you care for me like I care about you.*
>
> *I spend a part of my days baby, trying to figure out just how things got this way.*
>
> *I thought that we were in love, but I swear right now I don't know what you want.*
>
> *I make sure that I give you quality time. But lately I feel you're not home by design . . .*

Faith could not believe that Miles was sitting there in front of hundreds of people displaying his emotions on his sleeve. Silly girl, she thought, I'm probably the only one here who knows that those words are his personal testimony. As she looked around the audience, she could see that they received them as just pretty words. It made her feel special that she knew otherwise.

At that moment, she felt angry with Teri for not making it a priority to be here for such a special performance—or any other, in fact. This display of her man's talent would have made any woman proud. Heck, she was darn proud, and Miles was just her cousin!

The song came to an end and Faith was sad that such a delightful groove had to be over so soon. It was so easy to get lost in the sound, as she had done with her eyes closed, swaying. She was actually choreographing a dance in her head.

The audience roared, hooped, hollered, and even gave the group a standing ovation. Faith put her fingers to her mouth and gave a ballpark whistle. Giving the thumbs up, she yelled for more like the rest of the audience. At that moment, she could not help but think that Teri would be beside herself if she could see all of the love and adulation the audience poured out for his music.

Teri (Vanessa Williams) and Maxine (Vivica A. Fox) prepare for a feast.

The Joseph family partakes of Mother Joe's home cooking.

Michael Beach as Miles.

Lem (Mekhi Phifer) and Bird (Nia Long) celebrate their marriage.

Teri (Vanessa Williams) and Maxine (Vivica A. Fox) as bridesmaids.

Mother Joe (Irma P. Hall) and Ahmad (Brandon
Hammond) at the reception.

Vivica A. Fox stars as Maxine.

Man-to-man talk between Ahmad (Brandon Hammond) and Kenny (Jeffrey Sams).

Joseph sisters Bird (Nia Long), Teri (Vanessa Williams), and Maxine (Vivica A. Fox) share some woman-to-woman talk.

Vanessa Williams stars as Teri.

Mother Joe (Irma P. Hall) and her girls.

"Thank you. Thank you very much," Miles spoke to the crowd from the stage. "We're going to take a pause for the cause, and we'll be back in fifteen minutes with more Milestone." The audience applauded wildly.

When he looked into the crowd, he was surprised to see Faith waving to him. Dressed in a sheer, black-lace blouse and micro-mini skirt, she was looking quite beautiful, he thought, walking over to the bar where she had finagled a seat.

"That was the bomb!" Faith complimented, holding her cigarette for him to light. "I'm serious. You was jamming, Cousin! I didn't know you could play like that! You're good," she said, fully intending to extend a compliment well deserved.

"Thanks, but it's not all about me." Miles shrugged, a little embarrassed. "We're a group. Besides, the way they sing, they make my songs come alive," he said earnestly.

"Yeah, but you're the mastermind," she said, shaking salt onto her hand, downing a shot of Tequila, and biting into a lime. "You put it all together. This is your shit!" she said, as if trying to remind such a modest man. "Shit, the group is called 'Milestone.' It ain't called 'Them.'"

Miles chuckled. "'Them.' Hey, we were thinking about that name."

Faith wanted him to know just how well she had observed. "And you was working those keys like some early Stevie. You even got some Chick Corea chord progressions up in there. I like that."

Miles was impressed. "What do you know about Chick Corea?"

"Shit. Chick Corea, *Return to Forever*. Herbie Hancock, *Head Hunters*. Who wouldn't know that? C'mon Miles, I'm a dancer. I know my music."

They laughed, and Miles was actually surprised at her knowledge of music. Faith stared him square in the eyes and asked, "So you really wanna pursue your music full-time, huh? I think that'd be dope." She said it hoping it would be a vote of support.

Miles gave her a look that said, How did you know?

"I . . . I heard you and Teri talking," she admitted.

He didn't want to talk about Teri with Faith or anybody else, so he avoided the statement all together. "Your man is looking over here," he said instead.

Faith looked at the man she came with to Chic Rick's and turned back to Miles.

"Forget him. Family comes first," she said.

"He ain't gonna beat me up or nothin', is he?" Miles joked, just making sure.

"Please," she said with a "that-dude-ain't-beatin'-up-nobody" look. " 'Sides, I gotta get my career together before I think about a man. See, I got goals. Okay."

"Okay," echoed Miles.

"Promise you won't laugh . . . ?"

He laughed anyway, but he didn't mean to. It was more the type of laugh that slipped out because somebody asked you not to laugh.

She got a tiny bit insulted, because she was about to get serious. "Promise?" she asked again.

"I promise," he said, this time seriously, with no laugh.

"I wanna dance," she began dreamily.

Miles narrowed his eyes and was about to interrupt, because he thought that is what she did already.

"No," she continued, not letting him interject what she knew he was thinking, "I mean really dance. Do Broadway musicals, choreograph the Oscars . . . that kinda shit." She said it all looking as though she could already see her name up in lights.

"I've spent the last few years trying to figure out what makes me happy. After everything, I've learned the only thing that keeps me sane is dancing." She searched his eyes to see if he was following her. He was—Miles was an artist at heart. She had his attention for real now.

"So I'm gonna put every inch of my energy into it. So help me, Jesus," she said this with a show of conviction just short of doing a little sanctified shout and dance right there in the club.

Miles caught the feeling. "Hallelujah!" he said, raising his orange juice glass to her testimony, which sounded not much different from his own.

"And plus, it feels so damn good." She looked at him directly and saw he really understood. "You know what I mean? It's like that with you and your music, right?"

Miles was inspired by how much the two of them thought alike when it came to their artistry. He looked into her eyes and saw that they were definitely headed into unexplored territory. He did not trust himself to comment on the question presented, and instead asked, "You want a drink?"

"Hmm-hmm," she answered knowingly.

"You driving or is your man driving? I

don't want you getting drunk now." He had her laughing. Turning to the bartender, he said, "Sly, let me get another one, all right."

"You're crazy," she told him as she shook salt on her hand, downed the shot of Tequila, and bit the lime.

The club's DJ was playing music just as good as the band's sound in between the live sets. A Roy Ayer's tune came over the speakers and Faith grinned.

"Listen . . . That's my jam!"

"Your jam," said Miles as he sipped his orange juice. "Well, go'n and jam then."

Faith was already swaying in her seat, fingers snapping. She was lost in the music.

"Dance with me!" she said, jumping off of the bar stool and strutting seductively to the dance floor.

"I'm on my break," he shouted to her back.

"Come on," she summoned with her finger as she spun to face him.

Reluctantly, he looked at her already swaying on the floor. "Well, since you put it that way," he said out loud as if to convince himself.

On the small dance floor, they danced slow and close. She was clearly a professional, and her movements were precise and balletic. She could have easily been on stage at that very moment.

"You gonna do all that?" Miles asked over her shoulder, taking notice as to how lovely and staged her movements looked.

"If it feels right," she said, spinning back to face him. "Aw, you've got to let it go a little bit."

"Naw, I'm just doing the cool thing," he said, not trusting himself to let it go. Shit, he thought, we live in the same house. At the moment, one of them letting go was plenty.

11

ONLY TWO CUSTOMERS WERE IN BIRD'S Beauty Salon, and it was a welcome relief for the proud owner who had been doing so much hair that she could not see straight. Bird had just finished doing a press and curl, and Ahmad prepared her work area for the next customer.

Standing in the doorway, Simuel was cleaner than clean in a Versace suit and matching tie. Immediately, everyone turned to look at him. He never had to announce his arrival. Mr. St. James had learned early in life that when you showed up looking good and dressed to the nines, that was your announcement.

He walked toward Bird. "What's up, homes?" he said, turning to touch Ahmad's head.

Ahmad didn't speak. He didn't like that dude coming around bothering his auntie. He watched Simuel sit in the last salon chair, away from all of the others, and grin up at Bird. Ahmad went looking for the broom to arm himself—just in case.

"I knew you'd call," Simuel said, swinging the salon chair right and left.

"Let me take your briefcase," Bird said, sweetly playing the hostess with the mostest. She placed the briefcase on the work station, handed him a *Jet* magazine, and secured an apron around his neck.

"I'm gonna hook you up a free haircut." She asked, "What do you want? A fade around the edges, flat top?"

Simuel felt he had died and gone to heaven, and he certainly loved the generosity. "You have an orgasm thinking about me while you were giving a perm?" he asked her, being flip.

Bird thought she was almost sorry she

had called this fool, but she stayed cool. "I need a favor, Simuel."

Ah, Simuel thought, the moment he had waited for.

Ahmad watched as Bird asked Simuel for the favor. It would have been okay if that dude just did a friend a favor and kept moving, but no. Ahmad had seen the devious smile that crossed his face when Bird whispered in his ear. The first time he saw Mr. whatever-his-name-was at the wedding, Ahmad knew he was up to no good. That dude wanted his auntie bad and would do anything to get her. Damn, Ahmad thought, if Simuel's intentions were that obvious to him, everybody else must have known, too.

Bird finished asking Simuel for the favor. He smiled, nodding his head in an "I-can-do-this-for-you-baby" way.

"You know you got game, Bird," said Simuel as he perused her body. "So, what you gonna do for me?" he asked directly.

Bird stopped smiling. She was at a crossroads and she knew it. The favor that she had asked of Simuel was essential to her very existence. She had to make the right decision.

Ahmad was so mad, he was pacing the

floor. Something bad was gonna happen, he thought. He could feel it. He wished that Big Mama was out of the hospital. Why did his Aunt Bird have to go and ask that jerk for a favor, anyway? As far as he was concerned, all Simuel did well was wear some phat suits.

Miles was stuck in a traffic jam, but thanks to his Isley Brothers CD on full blast, he was grooving and feeling no pain. He casually looked across the street and saw Faith having an argument with a tall brother with dreadlocks.

The guy was Jamaican, in his late twenties, a real artsy type with a guitar slung over his back and chewing on a wooden stick. The argument between him and Faith persisted, and pedestrians began to stare.

Cars honked at Miles to move on since he had the green light. He contemplated whether to assist Faith or continue on his way. Looking back at the sidewalk, he saw the argument was getting hostile. The concerned cousin pulled over and walked up on a shouting match between the two.

"What's the problem?" Miles asked calmly.

Faith was shocked to see him. "I'm five minutes away from the biggest audition of my life, and this fool is trying to fuck me over!"

She dug into her bra, took out a ten-dollar bill, and gave it to the man. That made fifty dollars total that she had given him to play for her audition. He then got pissed off that she had more money than she led him to believe. Angrily, he balled it up and threw it at her, storming down the street.

"I'm gonna fuck you up, dread man!" she screamed behind him.

Miles watched Faith curse to herself. She closed her eyes and counted to ten so she could calm herself down. Just a little something she learned from Mother Joe.

Then, as if lightning had struck, she opened her eyes looking straight at Miles. "You can help me," she told him. "They got a piano in the audition room. You can play something and I'll just dance to it," she said hurriedly.

Miles threw up his hands in protest.

"Oh come on, cuz," she begged with no shame. "I need your help! This is important. I'm begging you. Please," she said and blinked her eyes once very slowly and deliberately, which allowed her long black lashes to spill onto her face.

◯   ◯   ◯

The large dance room had beautiful oak hardwood floors with giant windows facing the magnificent city skyline. Dressed in leotards and dance shorts, Faith was in the middle of the room stretching and getting into character.

She faced the three white casting directors and nodded that she was ready. Walking over to Miles, who was seated behind the old, perfectly tuned grand piano, she pushed the Play button on a cassette player. Miles was more nervous than Faith. He had never done anything like this before. It was almost as if he were auditioning.

Faith smiled as the beat began. It was a slow, moderate tune with a hip-hop flavor. Miles listened and began playing something bluesy. He watched Faith dance a slow modern jazz dance. She was beautiful on her feet. Her every move was precise and sensual. She had a rare ability to feel the music as she danced. Miles finally got comfortable behind the piano, improvising his music to Faith's moves. They complimented one another well.

As her moves became more intense, so did Miles, and they both finished to a grand finale. Faith was breathing intensely and her eyes were still closed as Miles's music ended. Slowly, her eyes opened and she turned to look at Miles. They were both proud. The casting directors watched. They said not one word—but that was what casting directors were trained to do. However, their faces said it all. They were impressed.

The front door opened, and Lem bolted in looking for his wife. "Bird," he shouted, as he entered into the well-illuminated house that was lit only by candlelight. He was surprised and bewildered at the same time. On the floor were flower petals that led to the living room.

"Bird, I have some great news!" he screamed excitedly, expecting to find her with every turn. When he entered the living room, he stopped when he saw Bird sipping a glass of champagne, dressed in pumps, a teddy, and an apron.

She handed Lem a glass and let him size her up. Damn, she looked good, he thought.

"I got a gig," he said, proudly sipping his champagne.

Bird clapped with excitement.

"Kenny called me yesterday and told me to ask about a job at the biggest in-house printing company in town," he said as he recounted the events that led to his hire.

"So I went in cold—they didn't know who the fuck Kenny Simmons was. So I knew I had to talk a big game." He said it proudly, for that had always been his forte.

"I told the man next to the man that I was the best man for the job. Finally, the boss looked at me and said, 'You're hired.' Right on the spot, like he knew that I knew that he knew I was his muthafuckin' man!"

Bird walked up to Lem and gave him a huge juicy kiss. Since he had lost his job, there had been no physical contact between them, so she was more than thrilled to be able to kiss him now.

Lem returned the kiss, but he still had the best part to tell. "With enough hours, I can get in the union. Then, we are talking serious bucks. We could get our own place," he dreamed as they clicked glasses to his new gig.

Bird took off her apron, gave him another fat kiss as she moved him over to the dining room, sat him in a chair, and straddled him.

Lem was totally worked up. He had a

vicious combination of emotional highs going on—the new job, the romantic setting, his wife whom he had not touched in weeks straddling him in practically nothing. Umph, he thought, where did he begin. The most powerful elixir of all was the champagne, which piled on a sensation all its own.

"Will that crazy-ass uncle of yours come down?" was the only question Lem had before he got started.

She grinned and shook her head no. Lem smiled and suddenly they both became animals. Bird ripped off his shirt and began unbuckling his pants. They were going at it full force before the chair went smashing to the floor. None of that slowed down the newlyweds in the least.

AT THE LARGE STATE-OF-THE-ART PRINTING company, many skilled, uniformed men and women worked behind their giant machines, and Lem was proud to be among them. The rumble of the machines was like music to him as he smoothly worked on a Carver press. It was obvious that he knew what he was doing. Papers flew through his machine easily.

The foreman walked over to talk to Lem. "I can't believe you finished the Johnson job. I didn't expect it finished until tomorrow." He reluctantly complimented him further by saying, "Good job."

LaJoyce Brookshire

Lem gave a nod of thanks.

"Hey," the foreman continued, "do you know how to run a four-and-a-half-by-nine Carver?"

Lem gave a look without trying to appear too cocky, "Yeah, I know how to work the Carver." And everything else in here, he wanted to add, but decided not to . . . yet.

The foreman checked his list approvingly. Lem beamed with the pride that is only found in knowing that a job is well-done. He continued working with a new confidence.

At lunch, Lem sat alone at a table eating a sandwich and staring out a window where a group of his coworkers were talking and smoking. Across the room, men in suits ate. Among the executives was Simuel. He noticed Lem sitting alone and walked over.

"Lem Davis? Simuel St. James," he said, holding out his hand. "Chief executive of sales and marketing."

Lem took the man's extended hand carefully, because he was smelly and dirty, totally opposite from the well-dressed man before him.

"The word is that you are fitting in nicely here," Simuel said, letting him know he had the 411 on his production.

"Shipping is making more deliveries on time. Of course, I heard you ain't bad with a machine, either."

"I'm no stranger to hard work," Lem said, uninterested in conversation with the brother who probably did not know what hard work was. So he went back to eating his sandwich.

"Well, that's good to know, because we always have more room for enthusiastic hard-working brothas, especially in the printing room." Simuel sized Lem up and down and was not impressed. What did Bird see in him, he pondered?

"You know, I'm not a stranger to hard work, either."

Here we go, thought Lem, some arrogant bullshit . . .

"Like you, Lem, I'm from the '*hood,* too."

Lem stopped chewing. He was offended by Simuel's comment. As he looked more closely, there was something vaguely familiar about him.

"I make $80,000 a year, because I was 200 percent better than everyone else, and I was always willing to sacrifice to get what I wanted."

Lem wasn't impressed—just hungry.

"That's why we *brothas* have to stick

together—pull one another up in a time of need. The white man ain't gonna do it. And soon it's gonna be your responsibility to help someone just like I helped you," said Simuel, spilling the beans.

Lem was confused enough to stop eating. "What are you talking 'bout?"

"I pulled some strings here to get you this job. Didn't you know?" he sneered.

Lem frowned. "Kenny Simmons referred me."

"Who?" Simuel asked, knowing full well who Kenny Simmons was.

The expression on Lem's face changed drastically. Beads of sweat lined the furrows in his bald head. Simuel clearly loved every minute of his little game.

"I know your wife, Bird. She asked me to hook you up a gig here in the print department."

Lem didn't want to believe what he had heard. Then, as if the fog had evaporated from his memory. "I remember you now. You were at my wedding reception."

"Yep," he said, then reminisced, "me and ol' Cola go way back."

"Cola?" Lem repeated, trying to remember if he had heard anybody call her that before.

"'Cola,' that's what we used to call Bird

back in the day, you know, since she had a body shaped like a Coca-Cola bottle." He grinned. "No disrespect, Lem, but I used to get more ass than a toilet seat—but I'll always remember your wife . . . She used to make a mothafucka want to scream."

Lem was fuming.

Simuel knew he had him by the balls, and he continued pushing his buttons. "So I'm glad your wife came to me in a time of need. See, I'm down for helping old friends, 'specially *brothas* trying to make something out of noth—"

Before he could finish, Lem grabbed a bottle and smashed it into his face. Simuel held his jaw in agony. Blood trickled down his chin. Then Lem hit him with a left hook. Simuel went down. Lem lost it then, and stomped Simuel like a crazy man, screaming, "You picked the wrong *brotha* to fuck with, mothafucka."

It took several other workers to break it up. Lem walked off.

Simuel screamed after him, "Yeah, well you can forget about your job, nigga!" His face was bruised and his $3,000 suit was stained with his own blood. He hurt all over and was pissed beyond the next millennium. But Lem was out of there.

◦   ◦   ◦

The front door of the salon burst open, slamming against the wall and shaking all of the mirrors, alarming everyone present, including Ahmad. Lem entered looking like an angry bull. He came to a halt when he saw Bird. She looked up and sensed trouble. Everyone went silent when he grabbed her arm right out in the open.

"Do you think I'm a fool?" he asked, shaking her.

"What?"

"I said, Do you think I'm some punk-ass mothafucka who don't know what time it is?"

The patrons all stared. Ahmad was nervous. Bird was embarrassed. In total shock, she pulled away and stormed to her office. Lem followed her and slammed the door so hard the place shook again.

"What the hell has gotten into you? This is my place of business!" she reminded him.

Oh, so it's your place of business, he thought as he knocked over paperwork, files, and boxes. Bird jumped back speechless as she watched her husband stare at her. Tears came to her eyes and the hurt was evident.

"You think I'm not even man enough to find my own fuckin' job!"

"I don't know what you are talking about," she lied.

"You know what the fuck I am talking about!"

Bird was furious that Lem knew the truth. "Baby, I . . . I was only trying to help," she stuttered. "I'm sorry."

"Sorry? Sorry for what? Strippin' my dignity? Or me finding out?" he demanded to know.

"Lem . . ."

"Are you fuckin' him?" he quizzed.

Tears flowed down her face and she shook her head no.

"What did you have to do for him, huh?" he said, grabbing her. "Ain't no nigga gon' give you a mothafuckin' thing free!" He knew this from first-hand experience.

"I only agreed to have dinner with him. That's it!" she said, fessing up.

"Bullshit."

"That was it," she wailed.

"Yeah," he said angrily as he reached to yank off the diamond bracelet from her wrist. "And what was this? Dessert?"

He threw the bracelet in her face and slammed Bird against the wall.

"I should have never taken this thing," she said as she burst into tears. "Simuel doesn't mean anything to me. I love you. It was only a piece of jewelry. I'm sorry." Now she was sobbing.

Lem stormed for the door. "Stay the fuck away from me!"

Bird wailed out in agony.

The shop was in chaos. Jada and Harome continually pounded on the locked bathroom door trying to persuade Bird to come out. After an hour had passed and she still did not respond, the employees were forced to call Teri to come to her rescue. They were worried, because all they could hear outside was her crying and vomiting into the toilet.

Teri arrived at the shop furious. How could that low-life scumbag do this to her baby sister? She knew it was against her better judgment to send for his tail from Joliet in the first place. She should have followed her first mind and let his little ass walk.

She suddenly got an idea and picked up the phone. ". . . No , I need you and your homies to do me a favor. No! I'm not pay-ing you $200, *not* after I got you a two-year parole for that car jacking last year. You owe me! Now take care of him!" she said seriously.

"And Blimp, *no guns*. I mean it!"

It was a quiet night down at Hamp's Tavern. The neighborhood bar that stood in the middle of the block had been a fixture on Fifty-third Street for years. There were a few customers watching a fight on the TV over the bar. Hamp, the owner and bartender, brought another drink to Lem, who had already had way too many. He had owned a bar for thirty years, and he knew how to assess when somebody had had too much. That somebody was Lem.

Hamp dialed the phone. "Yeah, Kenny? Hamp down at the bar. Look, get Bird. Lem's down here tying one on. Boy's tighter than virgin snatch."

Three large black men entered the bar looking like prison rejects. One of them was Blimp, and he was a biscuit away from 350 pounds, with a big, bald head to top it all off. His two boys watched his back as he looked around. Finally, Blimp saw Lem seated at the end of the bar and sat a couple of seats away from him.

"Gimme some of your best scotch,"

Blimp ordered Hamp. "An' leave the bottle
. . . he's payin'" Blimp said and pointed to
Lem when the bartender poured the shot
and left the bottle.

Lem was not in the mood for any non-
sense. What? Was this guy crazy? He didn't
even know him. So he just laughed it off.
"Yeah right."

Then, without any warning, Blimp
grabbed the bottle of scotch and smashed it
over Lem's head. Lem dropped to the
ground with blood spurting everywhere.
Although he was disoriented, he managed
to get up and throw a punch at one of
Blimp's goons.

Lem's blow forced the man backward,
crashing into a table where other customers
were drinking. Glasses shattered and a full-
out barroom brawl began.

Blimp and the men jumped on Lem as
he fought for his life. Hamp was through.
He screamed for them to take it outside,
but the fellas were all too oblivious to
Hamp's orders, and the fighting and curs-
ing continued.

Lem tripped one of the men, and as he
fell to the floor, Lem grabbed his arm and
twisted it until he yelled out in pain. His
shoulder was visibly dislocated.

Two down, one to go, Lem thought as he turned his focus to the freak who had started the whole mess. They went at one another until patrons ran screaming for the streets and Hamp was forced to call the police.

Lem was on the floor and beyond furious now. He didn't even know that dude. In a quick move, Lem pulled out his 9 millimeter from behind his back and pointed it at Blimp.

"Shit," said Blimp as he stomped his foot, "I knew I shoulda brought my gat!"

Lem got to his feet with fire in his eyes. He marched over and put the gun to Blimp's head. The other goon looked frightened.

"Whoever the fuck you are," Lem announced, "I will blow your fuckin' brains all over this bar."

"I'm Blimp—Mother Joe's brother's wife's nephew."

"I don't give a shit if you are kin, you goofy-lookin' mothafucka, I will kill you!" he screamed, temper escalating.

Lem pushed the gun to Blimp's temple and pushed him backward toward the bar. Blimp was literally shaking where he stood. He had totally underestimated the little guy.

Just beyond his temporary prisoner, Lem stole a glance of himself in the mirror. The reflection was not one that he liked to see . . . it was the old Lem Davis.

It took him a few seconds, but the realization that he had reverted back to his old self—even in the name of self-defense—was enough to force the gun to come away from Blimp's head. He just stared at his reflection feeling utterly defeated and completely disillusioned with life. Police sirens grew closer and closer.

Kenny's car pulled up in front of the bar just in time for him, Bird, and Ahmad to see the police lead Lem in handcuffs to the waiting police car. Blimp and his cronies were handcuffed, too.

Bird rushed over to the officers to try to persuade them to let Lem go. They forced her back. Lem was emotionless, facing the looks on his family's faces. He gazed sadly at Ahmad, who watched the police lead his uncle to the backseat of the car.

Kenny saw them stare at one another. "Ahmad, get back in the car!" he ordered.

Ahmad was frozen in his spot. He and Lem kept looking at one another. He watched sadly as the vehicle pulled off and disappeared down the street.

Bird was crying buckets of tears.

Damn, Ahmad thought, kickin' Simuel's ass, disturbing the peace, and carrying that gun . . . all of it landed Uncle Lem right back where he didn't wanna be—in jail.

Oh Big Mama, he thought, as a tear rolled down his face, what would you do?

13

SEATED AT HIS DINING ROOM TABLE, MILES enjoyed the solitude of his Sunday evening. Another week had come and nearly gone with no dinner at Mother Joe's. Even Miles had an eerily empty feeling without the weekly gathering. It just didn't seem right.

Playing with his Casio keyboard, he fiddled around with some lyrics and musical ideas. Someone entered the front door, forcing him to turn around.

Miles watched Faith come into the room and take off her coat. He noticed the tasteful lace bra hugging the skin beneath her blouse. When she turned, she caught him looking.

"Is Teri in?" she asked.

"She's at the hospital," he said, rewinding the cassette. "Wanna hear something?"

She was always game for good music. "Lay it on me."

A beautiful rhythm-and-blues track came up in need of lyrics, just before the piano solo began. Faith sat still, enjoying the melodic sounds. She closed her eyes and began to sway, inhaling the music. Miles watched her, caressing her with his eyes. He stopped the tape as Faith began smiling from ear to ear.

"That's beautiful," she said. "For your CD?"

"I don't know. Just a little something I'm messing with." He wasn't interested in talking about himself. "Hey, any news on your audition?"

An enormous smile that signaled "we did it" crossed her face as she squealed with delight. He jumped up and thrust his fists in the air.

"Come on. That's wonderful," he beamed, really proud of her.

Faith admitted, "Yeah, I'm pretty happy about it."

They roared with laughter, because they knew she was more than happy. "Ecstatic," "elated," and "overjoyed" would have all been better words.

"I was so scared," she admitted.

"You . . ." said Miles, who was really scared, because he had never done anything like that before, and because there was so much riding on his performance for her that he didn't want to blow it.

"I gave my two-week notice at the firm."

Faith knew what a real milestone that was for him. A true test of faith, in himself and in his marriage.

She jumped up and hugged him. "When your CD drops, you're gonna blow up, Miles. It's just the beginning. Let's celebrate. Wanna beer?"

A few beers later, they sat cozily near the fireplace, both a bit tipsy and both very comfortable.

"Here's to 'Leaps of Faith.' Get it?" she asked.

"I get it. To 'Leaps of Faith.'"

"I'm moving out this weekend, Miles," she said regretfully. "Me and Teri under the same roof just ain't working. Teri's tough."

How well did Miles know that. "So you're letting her run you out of here."

147

"Yes, but then again I need my own space. I'm always on the go. And I can't stay in one place for too long . . ." she said, sipping her beer. His eyes were scanning every inch of her.

"My mama died when I was ten, and I've been on the go every since. You know, my daddy had five kids from five different women. And he was always on the go." She said it wishing once again that she could have seen more of him.

"Guess I inherited that from him. I've lived with stepsisters, stepmothers, aunties, uncles, cousins . . ."

Miles thought she had turned out incredibly to have been through so much. "You've stayed with all of them," he said staring into her eyes.

She could not help but stare back. "Yeah, I've worn out quite a few welcome mats. But we all cool. There's no hostilities or anything like that." She didn't want to add that this was with the exception of Teri.

Plainly, she concluded, "When it's time to go, it is time to go."

"That's bullshit," he said so intensely it rattled her.

"Excuse me?"

"That's a lonely life. You should stop pretending you don't need anybody."

Faith tried to play him off. She was not ready to venture in this conversation with him or anybody else. She looked at his face and noticed his few gray hairs. For the first time, she felt their age difference. She saw his wisdom.

"Shit, why am I here wasting my time when you ain't hearing me."

Faith could not help herself. She reached out and gave Miles a hug. They had shared a lot and had come a long way in understanding one another. Then she kissed him. Even though he shook his head no, something else was saying yes.

She leaned forward for a better angle to kiss him again. He was hesitant. They stared at one another for a moment before she gently kissed him again. Each kiss was deeper and more passionate than the one before.

She moved over him hungrily, arching her body over his. As her eyes told him how much she craved him, she led him toward the window. With a magnificent view of Chicago behind them, they kissed one another as if it were the last either of them would ever have.

His hands went up her dress, and he ripped off her panties as she unzipped his pants. They clawed like two people in desperate need of one each other. She gasped in ecstasy as he entered her.

Teri and Ahmad walked from the elevator down the hallway to the front door. She found her keys and unlocked the door. Upon entering the apartment, she dropped the keys. As she bent to retrieve them, she stopped dead in her tracks at the sight she saw in her living room.

There was her husband and her cousin making love unabashedly and oblivious to anything or anybody else—including her.

She was drained of all emotion. It was as if all of the life had been sucked from her body with each of their strokes. Momentarily pinned in her spot, she picked up her keys and grabbed her nephew, forcing him back out of the door.

"What's wrong, Aunt Teri?" Ahmad asked from where he was lingering in the hallway. "Can't I spend the night?"

She was trembling so much she could not answer. "No," she finally said, slowly trying to stop herself from bursting into tears. "We're going back to your mom's."

Ahmad looked back toward the condo to try to get a glimpse, but Teri grabbed him before he could see anything. The last thing she needed was for him to see Miles and Faith that way.

The cousins-in-laws climaxed together. They were not cognizant that anyone had ever been there. Miles moved away from Faith disconcerted, dazed. They were both overcome with intense feelings about what had just occurred.

Faith pulled herself together, putting on her clothes quickly and searching for her underwear. Miles left the living room hurriedly—in a desperate attempt to be somewhere . . . anywhere that Faith was not. She saw him scrambling to get away from her and lowered herself onto the couch, not blaming him, but spiting herself.

The knock on Maxine's kitchen door interrupted her decorating. Peeking out the door, she saw it was Teri with Ahmad standing there. "Hey," Maxine said with

151

her usual perkiness, opening the door wider so they could enter, "I was just getting stuff ready for our anniversary party tomorrow."

Teri did not say anything. She just came in and looked at Maxine, who then saw her sister's tear-stained face. She did not care how much dissension was between them recently, Teri was her sister and nobody and nothing was going to make her cry.

"What's wrong?" Maxine said, sensing it was something other than Mother Joe.

Teri shook her head, still unable to speak—still unable to smile. Sitting down with a distant look, she was clearly perplexed.

Pouring a cup of coffee for her, Maxine thought twice about giving it to her plain and went to the cabinet for her stash of brandy.

Teri accepted the remedy for all problems tearfully. "Can I stay here tonight? And don't ask me any questions," she warned, sending a loud signal that she would talk only when she was ready.

Maxine knew that something must have been seriously wrong for her to ask a favor. She acknowledged finally that it would be fine for her to stay and that her privacy would be kept. Teri sipped her brandy-laced coffee in thoughts so ocean-deep it looked as if she were about to drown.

T HOSE WHO GATHERED IN CELEBRATION OF
Maxine's and Kenny's eleventh anniversary
applauded loudly when they blew out the
candles on the cake. The party had plenty of
music, food, and drink—all of the ingredients for a good house party.

Ahmad and Kelly danced together,
mocking their parents, who looked like two
kids in love. Jada, the manicurist from
Bird's shop, did an intense grind on the
shortest and skinniest man at the party. The
crowd snickered at her 200-plus-pound

body jiggling all over the tiny man, who's face was secured snugly in her boobs. A sight for all to see, but not a complaint was made from either participant.

Teri stood at the top of the stairs with her fifth vodka and orange juice of the evening. Prepared to drink another if necessary, she was still tense—a ticking time bomb ready to explode. She was not in a party mood, and it showed. She stayed in the shadows where she could be seen just enough to claim that she was present and accounted for. The more she saw everyone else having a good time, the more she became depressed.

Kenny and Maxine danced slowly together through all of the songs—fast and slow. Teri could see the love and chemistry still sparking between them and flashed back to her brief relationship with Kenny. Looking at the couple, Teri realized their magic was something she and Kenny had never possessed. In fact, she thought, she could accurately say "magic" was an emotional height she had never attained with anyone.

Looking around, Teri zeroed in on Faith playing cards. She could not believe the tramp was still hanging around. Hadn't she stayed in town long enough? Wasn't she antsy for a new conquest, since she already had one old fool in town?

Teri was still seething over what she saw. If the chick would just disappear, then she could pretend she didn't see them pretending nothing had happened. Taking a visual tour of the room as she descended the stairs, Teri heard Miles singing to the music with some friends.

Harome saw her looking at him and sashayed over. "Gotta admit, the boy is good." Teri gave him a "yeah right" glare.

Harome didn't let her attitude interfere with the information he felt compelled to deliver. "Dwayne Johnson, my client who works with Miles, told me the chile's quittin' his job for his music," he finished, snapping his fingers.

Teri was stunned. The look on her face indicated it was the first time she had heard any such thing as foolish as Miles quitting his job. She bolted for the kitchen with new steam pouring from her ears.

As they continued their slow drag, the kiss that Kenny gave his wife was a decoy for the mannish act he had planned. He grabbed a handful of her butt like he used to do when they were younger and watched her squeal with delight. After three children, Maxine was still as much of a fox to him as the day they met. She made it easy to love her. There was no such thing as Maxine letting herself go—secretly, she was way too vain.

WHY DON'T YOU GET THE FAMILY together in the kitchen so we can talk 'fore everyone gets too drunk," she whispered to Kenny above the music.

The minute Kenny left to complete his roundup, Ahmad popped the biggest question of the evening, "Hey, Mom? Wanna dance?"

She could not resist the request of her miracle child, and they proceeded to take advantage of the great music pumping full-blast through the speakers. Ahmad had developed a good sense of movement from his mother, and the two of them rocked in tandem to the beat. The guests formed a crowd around the mother and son duo and began to chant, "Party over here! Party over here!"

Kenny entered the kitchen and saw Teri standing alone amid the food and yet another full drink, crying. "Are you okay?" he asked, walking toward her.

She looked at him with her eyes full of tears. Tears that had been held in all her life. She reached up, hugged him tightly, and rested in the comfort of his embrace. Kenny felt terribly nervous and held her away at arm's distance.

The simple action snapped Teri back to reality. She turned away from him and found comfort in her drink instead. "All these years—and I still envy what you and Max have," she said as an apology for her behavior.

"I always thought if you and I had gotten married, my life would've been different. But it wouldn't. I'd've found a way to screw it up," she said, her voice full of sorrow.

The family members filtered into the kitchen one by one, leaving the party in the living room in full swing.

"Mama's medical bills are coming in, and they're ridiculous," Maxine said, hating to hold such a heavy discussion in the middle of her party. "Now we all knew health insurance wouldn't cover the whole hospital bill."

"So between the five of us," Kenny picked up, "we need to pitch in so we can take care of this tonight."

Each lost in their own thoughts, no one responded immediately.

Bird got a bright idea. "What about that cash Mother Joe's supposedly got stashed?"

"That's just a stupid myth. There's no money!" Maxine said incredulously. How could she even suggest such a thing for bills that needed to be paid now. Maxine had a bright idea of her own, "Teri, you have more money than all of us. Maybe you and Miles can pay the hospital bill and we can—"

"No," Teri interrupted, putting up a finger for Maxine to hold that ridiculous thought. "You will not run that game on me again. . . . Not again."

Ahmad wandered into the kitchen, but the adults were too engrossed in their conversation to notice him. He made himself invisible while he listened and watched his

Aunt Teri pour herself another drink. He noticed that she had not talked to anyone all night. And he also noticed that she was on her seventh drink, from what he had counted. What was up with her? he thought.

Teri then, cruelly and coldly, came up with bright idea number three. "We can pay Mama's hospital bill by selling the big house."

Everyone was dumbstruck. Teri had made some brilliant money making moves in her life, but that suggestion was the most selfish statement she had ever made.

"We are *not* going to sell something Mama and Daddy took their entire life to build and pay for," Maxine told her.

Teri stared at each family member before speaking. "Don't you freeloaders realize nobody's paying utilities or taxes on that house but me," she told them, slamming her drink down on the counter. "And crazy-ass Uncle Pete belongs in a home like everyone's been talking about for years."

Bird gasped. "Mama would kill us for putting Uncle Pete in a home."

"Mama . . . is incapacitated!" Teri screamed at them, trying to reason. "That's why I'm selling the house!"

"We are *not* selling the house!" Maxine jumped in.

"*I'm* guardian of her estate," Teri informed and then defined the legalese, "that means, *I* make the decisions!"

Miles interjected, "Teri, maybe you should reconsi—"

Bird smelled trouble. "I say we vote . . ."

"Bullshit! The last time we voted, you two voted that bitch"—Teri screamed, pointing in the living room—"in my house, and she fucked my husband! Yeah, that's right. Faith fucked my husband," Teri pronounced the words, glad to finally have gotten her secret off of her chest.

Everyone looked at Miles in shock. Ahmad gasped. So did Harome, who was eavesdropping at the door. Now Ahmad knew why Aunt Teri had been acting so funny since the night they went to her condo. He just wanted to run over to her and tell her everything would be all right, but she was so mad—like a crazy woman— he didn't dare touch her.

Miles was horrified that she knew, and it left him struggling for words, "Teri . . . I . . . i-it just happened. It didn't mean anything . . ."

Teri lost it. She grabbed a butcher knife from the rack and lunging toward Miles. He jumped back just in time. Bird and Maxine ran to restrain Teri, but she found an open-ing and kept moving, looking for any and every opportunity to kill his ass.

Chasing him into the living room, Teri had him trapped behind a table. The guests screamed when they saw her with the knife at Miles's heels. She lunged for him again and ripped his shirt.

"Ahmad!" Maxine yelled, "get your little cousins and the rest of the kids and go upstairs to your room! Now!"

Ahmad reluctantly did as he was told, thinking to himself, get him, Aunt Teri.

Teri suddenly changed courses. Her seek-and-destroy mode flipped to Faith. When Faith saw Teri's attention turn to her, she immediately started screaming.

Faith jumped into the midst of the guests for safety, but Teri was hot on her heels and swiped the blade through the air at her. Faith kept moving, thinking all the while, She knows. How did she find out? Jumping onto the couch and then the refreshment table—forcing the punch, cake, and cookies to the floor—did not stop Teri from following Faith's every move. Faith may have been ten years Teri's junior, but the older cousin proved to be just as nimble. It was the fury of a scorned woman that was

Teri's driving force. It propelled her blindly.

Kenny rushed over and jumped on Teri, crashing into the stereo before she conceded. The guests watched in silence. Teri trembled, crying. Everyone looked at Miles. What could he say? Finally, Miles gathered his things and left.

Faith watched him leave, wanting to go with him, but not daring to take sides against the family. She sat there staring into space, feeling lost and alone and wondering about Miles's fate. Her focus was interrupted by Teri standing in front of her. Tears streamed down Faith's face as she trembled in fear of the woman who had just tried to kill her husband in public.

Teri was exhausted and embarrassed, but she had one more thing to get out of her system. "Get out of this house," she told Faith. "And get out of my condo."

Faith shook in the quake of Teri's anger. Tears ran down her face. She was rigid as Teri backed her up against a wall.

"I said get out!" Teri commanded.

Crying uncontrollably, Faith refused to leave.

Teri took a deep breath in a "let-me-try-this-one-more-time-'cause-I'm-two-seconds-off-of-your-ass" tone. *"Get out!"*

Teri shouted, just short of rolling up her sleeves.

"I can't!" Faith said tearfully. "I got nowhere else to go!" She slid down the wall, dissolved in tears, in total embarrassment for what she had done with Miles and in admission of her need to be loved by family.

The clan now understood why Faith had come back to Chicago. Ahmad looked around at his broken family from the top of the stairs and cried a fit of tears in his heart. Oh Big Mama, what to do? What to do? was his only thought.

16

AHMAD HAD BEEN SITTING AT THE SIDE
of Mother Joe's bed for hours holding
her hand. Recently, the hospital had
been the only quiet place in Ahmad's
world. He came there regularly to think,
get some peace, and be with Mother Joe.
He had not given up on the thought that
one day she would wake up. And when
she did, he fully intended on being
there.

It had been five weeks since Mother Joe
had been in a coma. In that very short

period, every grown person in Ahmad's family had gone crazy.

A slight movement on the bed snapped him to attention. His mouth dropped as Mother Joe's eyes slowly opened. He smiled and his heart leaped for joy. He knew it! He absolutely knew she would wake up someday.

Mother Joe swallowed and tried to focus. Looking over at Ahmad, she smiled and noticed the roses from her garden on the night stand. They, too, brought a smile to her lips. With the tube in her mouth, it was difficult for her to speak.

Ahmad put a finger to her lips. "Don't try to talk."

Mother Joe swallowed again and tried anyway with great difficulty. "You were here with me, weren't you?"

"Yeah," he said proudly.

Mother Joe smiled at her Sweet Pea. He had always brought her so much joy, never causing any trouble, always being a help to her. She knew that if anyone would be next to her when she woke up, it would be Ahmad, so it did not surprise her in the least that he was there.

"A lot of bad things happened while you were away, Big Mama. Everyone was worried about you. But not me. I knew you'd come around," he admitted. "I love you, Big Mama."

She smiled and tilted her head to beckon him to her. She whispered something very special in his ear. He listened intently to her instructions and grinned in approval. Then she kissed him sweetly.

Struggling with her words, she murmured, "I'm tired, baby. My soul is tired. So I need you to do something for me . . . only you can," she said, stressing her point.

"I need you to . . ." She coughed. "I need you to . . ." Before she could finish, Mother Joe had a coughing fit. The tube in her throat had filled with liquid and was choking her.

Ahmad panicked. "Big Mama," he said as he poured water. She didn't want to drink. Mother Joe needed to talk to him and she wanted to talk to him now.

Her coughing became harsher and raspier, until it was uncontrollable. The heart and lung monitors beeped rapidly and Ahmad became frightened. His eyes filled with tears.

A nurse entered with the doctor to assist Mother Joe. Another nurse gathered Ahmad's things and forced him to leave the room. She closed the door in his face while they attended to the coughing patient.

Ahmad stood at the door, peering in on the scene for some time. He had hopes of going back in and picking up their conversation where she had left it. His heart thumped in anticipation of the doctor's reviving his Big Mama so they could conclude their little talk.

After several minutes with the doctors behind closed doors, he dropped his head and realized that he had better come back another day. Then his head popped up abruptly as if pulled by some force. He looked into Mother Joe's room and saw that all of the machines had stopped beeping and buzzing. Ahmad's tears flowed freely in grief for his grandma.

Reverend Williams said a prayer as the bronze casket covered with flowers was slowly lowered into the open grave. Harome and Jada were among several mourners besides the immediate family who stood there numb. They were all cried out.

Ahmad watched the casket settle in its permanent spot in the ground and looked around at his family. Everyone was avoiding the eyes of the others, safely choosing to watch the casket.

Finally, a tear slid down Ahmad's face as he thought, It's up to me now . . .

Maxine was coming up the walk to Mother Joe's house when she stopped dead in her tracks in front of the FOR SALE sign she saw on the lawn. She took off her sunglasses to get another look without the tinted glass blocking her view.

She mumbled to herself, totally outdone, "Mama ain't lukewarm in the ground and the girl got her shit for sale."

She stormed furiously into the house. Teri had her nerve, she thought. As if selling the house was exclusively her decision. As if none of them had ever lived there. As if the house had not one ounce of sentimental value. Clearly, it was nothing but a cash transaction to Teri or she wouldn't have pulled her little stunt.

Making her way to the kitchen with all of those thoughts rambling through her mind, Maxine missed something in the dining room. She opened cabinets and started pulling down items to cook and then stopped, thinking that she had, in fact, seen something strange on her way to the kitchen.

Peering out of the swinging door slowly, she did a double-take at the vision before her. "Oh my God! Uncle Pete . . . ? You're out of your room." She was shocked.

Uncle Pete sat calmly at the dining room table in an old robe as if he sat there every day. He had grown bald, save for a few uncombed gray hairs and a long gray beard.

"We going to the creek today, Joe?" he asked, staring into space.

Maxine thought, Oh goodness, he thinks I'm Mama.

"We can catch some trout for dinner, put it in the iron pot with some butter," Uncle Pete continued, completing his thought, which brought water to his mouth in anticipation of the meal he desired.

Glancing over at the photo on the piano of Uncle Pete and Mother Joe holding up a fish when they were much younger back in Mississippi, Maxine realized that he was living the past as if it were today.

"No, Uncle Pete. I'm Maxine! Mama is gone!" she said with frustration and emotion creeping into her voice. "She's dead!"

Uncle Pete became agitated, shaking his head vehemently. He sat silently for a moment before he once again forced the conversation to a time only in his mind.

"Remember, Daddy would raise hogs, gut 'em, cure 'em, then cut up the meat in brine, then put it in the smoke house for sausages . . . ooh wee." He forced himself to remember that wonderful time from the past, but his hand shook uncontrollably at the news he had just received.

Uncle Pete still believed Mother Joe was standing behind him. "Daddy's gone now, so you have to take care of me, Joe," Uncle Pete told her.

Maxine's eyes filled with tears, and a shiver went up her spine. It was her turn to take over the family. It took Uncle Pete's bewilderment for her to realize it. Recognizing her responsibility once and for all, Maxine wiped the tears from her eyes, stood erect, and gave a welcome sigh to the new role she was to play as a Joseph family member.

The restaurant overlooking the Chicago River was bustling with its usual lively lunch crowd. Maxine and Bird were seated at a small table waiting for Teri.

"What time did you tell her to be here," Maxine said, looking at her watch.

"I told her two o'clock. Don't worry, she'll show," Bird said calmly, just as Teri walked into the restaurant. "Teri, over here."

Taking off of her coat, Teri said, "Sorry, I'm late. What's up?"

Maxine had planned the little meeting, so she felt it was her duty to speak up. "Teri, look now, I know you are mad at the world for what happened to you and Miles." She said it gently, trying not to be confrontational even though she was referring to the sale of the house. "But you are blaming and hurting the rest of the family."

"And who's gonna pay her bills," Teri glared at Bird, "*you?*"

Bird put her head down, because she had not met the payment schedule as she and Teri had agreed upon, even though business was good. Bird had used her money instead to keep them afloat when Lem was not working.

Teri dug into her purse and tossed an envelope on the table. "This is Mama's living will. I'm the executrix, and I've already filed the petition. I've got Mama's medical records."

But Maxine was ready. "See Teri, I knew you would do something like that. So," she said digging into her purse, "I went to Kenny's lawyer and I drew up a motion to cease and desist. And I guarantee you, we are going to stop the sale of Mama's house."

Bird beamed proudly at Maxine.

Teri was in shock. "That's fine," she said, taking out a fifty-dollar bill and throwing it on the table to pay for the lunch they had yet to order.

"Aw Teri, don't be like that. Don't leave," Bird pleaded.

Maxine calmly sipped her coffee and watched her sister leave.

"I've gotta go to the bathroom," Bird said, agitated.

Bird was doubled over the toilet, vomiting. Her stomach was so upset all of the time now. She came out of the stall to rinse her mouth and splash cold water on her face. Maxine felt that Bird had been in the bathroom far too long and finally got up from the table to check on her.

Bird was walking down the hallway still feeling queasy when she saw Maxine.

"Honey, are you okay?"

"Lem's gonna be a father," Bird confessed.

"You're the fish in Mama's dream," Maxine realized.

Bird nodded tearfully. "I miss him so much, Max."

"I know, Bird," she said, holding out her arms. Bird welcomed the sisterly love. "But you can't call your ex to help your husband find a job behind his back. A man has to be a man. You can't take that away from him. If you do, he has nothing." She held Bird so they could be eye-to-eye.

"Just like with Mama when Daddy went and gambled all the money away. She didn't make him feel like a loser going behind his back. She just worked hard, sacrificed, and got the job done—left Daddy his dignity," she said, smoothing her hair. "Men need that, baby."

The words of wisdom were well received, and Bird's spirits soared. "I wish I could be like you, Max. And deep down, so does Teri."

"No. I'm nothing but a housewife and mother with three kids, and their bad asses," Maxine joked. "I-I look at you and your shop—the head for business you have—Teri and her accomplishments, and I ask myself, what am I here for?"

"You're here for us to lean on," admitted Bird, giving her sister a big hug.

"Thank you, baby. But I'm gonna be an auntie," she sang, guiding her back to the dining room. "Now we've got tons of things to do for the baby . . ."

MILES WAS IN A STATE-OF-THE-ART recording studio, doing with his life exactly as he had promised—recording his debut CD. He and the band were in a soundproof booth cutting tracks over and over. The melodic sounds had everyone who worked at the studio swaying. They sounded so good that people in other sessions came to listen to Milestone do their thing.

Ahmad was with the engineers who adjusted the knobs and worked to ensure that the sound being recorded was perfection.

This recording environment was really cool, he thought, enjoying the whole process.

After the track was finished, Miles called a break and lit a cigarette. Two of the band members lingered behind to compliment him on the song.

"I think that was the one, man," raved Jo-Jo.

"No, man. We need to do this shit again," said K.C., who was even more of a perfectionist than Miles. They knocked fists with their bandleader and left the booth to enjoy the twenty-minute break that was strictly enforced.

Miles spotted Ahmad and went into the engineering booth. He loved this little kid. He had more stamina and determination than anybody he ever knew at that age. In Miles's opinion, Ahmad was the real star in the family. It would only be a matter of time . . .

"Sounding good, Uncle Miles."

"Thanks, man. Glad you could make it."

"I'm glad I could, too," Ahmad said, hoping not to sound too eager. "After all, its been tough, what with school, workin' at the shop afterward—and trying to coordinate what to do with all that loot Big Mama left me."

Miles's eyes widened. "Loot? What loot?"

Ahmad was truly a brilliant child. Carefully following the instructions given to him by Mother Joe and then throwing in his own pepper to the gumbo, he left the recording studio after laying the same rap on Miles that he would later give to Teri, Bird, and Faith.

Being such a good student of character analysis, Ahmad had estimated correctly what each of the responses of the family members would be.

Ahmad always listened carefully to everything that Mother Joe told him, and the one thing she said was to pay close attention to a person's character. That way, when you need to go to them for something, you will know just how to do it.

Ahmad was getting a haircut when he hooked in his Aunt Bird.

"*Cash?*" she questioned, totally interested.

With Bird, he knew he had to make the story sound as juicy as that gossip she thrived on every day.

"The day she died, see, I was the only one at the hospital. And Big Mama told me where she stashed some money for me none of y'all know nothin' about," he said as he looked into the mirror at Bird to see if his plan was working.

Shock was written all over Bird's face. Oh yeah, it was working.

Faith was on a break from rehearsal at the dance studio. Ahmad sat on a high stool as he calculated just how to appeal to her enormous and worldly ego.

Faith had no shame in questioning, "You mean dead presidents? How many you talkin' 'bout?"

"Lots. I mean beaucoup," Ahmad stressed. "Enough for college. See, you're well traveled, Faith, and I'm thinkin', maybe *you* could help me figure out what to do with the dough."

Faith grinned, her mind racing. She even did a double pirouette in her heart at the prospect of Ahmad even coming to her for advice.

Ahmad silently smiled inside.

Sitting at the head of the large conference table, Ahmad overlooked the Chicago skyline while appealing to his Aunt Teri in the language that she understood well—money.

"Are you sure this *isn't* the money from the will?" Teri inquired, trying to pinpoint the what, when, and where of it all. She thought she knew everything there was to know about her mother's estate, so to hear that there was money elsewhere rendered her suspicious.

Ahmad acknowledged that he was certain this was money that even she knew nothing about. "Aunt Teri, you're the smartest in the family," he said, beginning his manipulation. "If I was your son, wouldn't you invest it for my future? Do the right thing for the family?"

Ahmad could see her clearly thinking about that for a moment. He went in for the kill. "See, I figure if you help me, I could give you a third—like a fee—then you could pay Big Mama's bills without selling her house."

The calculator in Teri's head worked overtime. Ahmad could see her counting to herself as he thought, Gotcha!

Continuing his pitch to the new full-time musician, Ahmad knew Miles would easily become a player if the musical side of him were considered. "And I'd give you a percentage if you help me invest it—then maybe you can use the money to promote your new CD!"

Miles had just begun his search for investors in the Milestone project, and he could not believe that one of the youngest members of his very own family had made him an offer. Thank you, Lord, he said to himself silently.

"You told anyone else about this?" he asked Ahmad, fully intending not to put the name Teri with "anyone else," but meaning the same.

Ahmad knew first-hand from working in the salon that Bird wanted nothing more than to pay Teri back and get out from under her clutches. "No, Aunt Bird, I haven't told anyone else about this. But I'd be willing to give you some of it and you could pay off Aunt Teri's loan . . ."

Bird's eyes twinkled.

Bird's business had been going well, and she was so pleased to see her dream manifested. The only bad aspect of her business was Teri breathing down her neck every second about the decisions she made. Granted, if it were not for Teri's money, Bird knew there would never have been a Bird's Beauty Salon. But if Teri wanted to go into the beauty business, then she should have opened her own place.

Most families have similarities that peg them as being related, but Ahmad never realized until he came face-to-face with each of them in his little manipulation game how much the Joseph clan was alike.

Each of the family members asked him the very same question, "Ahmad, why don't you tell me where the money is?" He knew he had all of them. Teri, Miles, Bird, and Faith all fell in step hook, line, and sinker. Ah, he thought, thanks Big Mama. That character thing really worked. Ahmad's plot was a winner; it was sweeter than the honey on a honeycomb.

Of course, he agreed to tell each of them where the money was located. It gave him the most pleasure to announce the day, place, and time. "Sunday at three. At Big Mama's." All agreed.

Maxine and Ahmad walked by Lake Michigan on a picturesque day with just a hint of a breeze blowing in the Windy City. Ahmad was wearing his basketball uniform under his coat. He swung on the monkey bars while his mother sat in front of him, still filled with excitement from the good game he played.

"I tell you Ahmad, and that last steal. The way you pulled it out and scored those two points . . . ooh wee!" she said, downright proud of her big baby.

"I know," he quipped. "They heard you scream 'That's my baby' in Jamaica."

Maxine laughed. "Well, I don't care what you say, I was proud of you."

Ahmad grinned and thought he had better start up his plan again. He needed to be extra careful. This was his Mama he faced, not some relative he saw once a week. He needed to tread very carefully in order to get his mother to play along with him. One thing was for sure, he could not tell his parents about the money. So he had to find another way.

"Mama, think I could have a victory dinner?"

"Baby, you can have anything you want."

"Think I could have lima beans and neck bones, greens with hot sauce, hot cakes, and some fried chicken?"

"A'ight, you're entitled. 'Sides, I haven't cooked like that since . . ." She drifted off, thinking that it had been some time since she prepared a meal like that. Mother Joe was alive then, and she did not want to drag herself into that depression in the midst of Ahmad's victory plans.

"Yeah, sure. When?" she asked.

"Sunday? At Big Mama's?" he suggested. Ahmad tried not to flinch when he saw his mother's eyes narrow. When she did that, it meant she sensed something fishy was going on.

"You're up to something," she told him in a motherly voice.

"Huh?" he questioned, faking his innocence.

Maxine was not to be fooled that easily. "Boy, I carried you for nine months and went through . . ."

Ahmad knew this drill and recited it with her. "Twenty-three hours, forty-five minutes, and ten seconds of labor, cleaned your butt while your little ding-a-ling peed in my face . . ."

Maxine had to laugh. This kid of hers was some mess. When their laughter died down, she would not let her point rest.

"So Mama knows when you're up to

something," she wanted him to know. "You're trying to get everyone together for Sunday dinner."

Ahmad gave in. "Big Mama wants me to. I think it's what she was tryin' to tell me before she died."

Maxine believed him without another word and fell silent.

Teri sat in the conference room staring out the window at the view of the city. It was her favorite room in the building, for it appeared as if the city were at her feet and she could touch the sky. She was using her lunch break to think instead of eat—that always seemed to do her body good.

So much had happened to her recently, to her family—the people in the world she cared about most. A few of the things that had happened, she sadly realized, were her fault. Teri resolved that this would be the day she would undo some things she had done.

Looking at the phone a moment, there was one thing she knew she could take care of immediately. She dialed and shook herself from the emotional wreck she had been when she stepped into the room. Back into Miss Teri, business as usual.

"Yes, Jonathan Oliver, please. It's Teri Joseph . . ."

18

SUNDAY AFTERNOON ARRIVED CLOUDLESS, sunny, and bright. Mother Joe's kitchen was once again well-stocked in preparation for the family dinner. Fresh produce was piled in one side of the sink and steam from the pots on the stove filled the air.

Preparing the dinner was a family effort. Maxine was sweating as she rolled out the dough for dumplings at one end of the counter. Kenny chopped onions as he held back the tears on the other end. Ahmad stirred a pitcher of Kool-Aid while Kelly liberally added the sugar.

"Kelly, don't put too much sugar in there now," Kenny warned, "you'll be bouncing all over the walls."

Bird entered through the back door and was surprised to see Maxine in the kitchen cooking. "Hey."

"Hey," Kenny said.

"What y'all doin' here?" Bird asked.

"Oh, we're just cooking a little Sunday dinner," he said, continuing to chop. Maxine smiled knowingly.

"All right," Bird said, shooing Kenny out of the way, "let the ladies take over."

"Oh yeah, after all of the hard work is over you want to come in now and take over."

Maxine knew Kenny was only helping because she had asked. Now that he was asked to leave, he would gladly do so. He wiped his hands quickly.

"That's right," Maxine said, relieving him from his duties as he stepped behind her to kiss her neck, "you can go work hard in there with the remote control and watch football."

"I can do that?" he asked as he kissed her, making sure he had permission.

"Uh-huh."

"You sure?"

"Yeah, I'm sure."

"You don't need anything?"

"No, thank you."

Kenny ran out of the kitchen a happy man.

"You want me to start the dumplings?" Bird asked, eager to help.

"All right," Maxine conceded. "But you watch your measuring. You know how you are," she said, turning to the stove to get a pan from the hanging rack.

Bird whispered behind Maxine's back, pointing in Ahmad's face, "Why didn't you tell me they were gonna be here. I'm gonna kick your butt."

Ahmad maintained a look of total innocence as he stirred the Kool-Aid. Bird scooped the flour like nothing had happened when Max turned back.

"Ahmad, why don't you put the Kool-Aid in the refrigerator. And after you do that, why don't you start me some water for the turnip greens, okay?" Maxine directed. "Thank you." She doled out orders in the kitchen as easily as Mother Joe had. It was both comforting and scary to her that she moved into her new role so easily.

Kelly helped her mom pour cornmeal into the bowl for the catfish. Ahmad was busily licking the chocolate cake batter from his fingers when the doorbell rang. Maxine never looked up. Bird was curious about who else would now be present. It was Teri.

"Hey," greeted Bird as she leaned to one hip, totally surprised and pleased to see her.

Teri kissed Ahmad and smelled the air, going directly to the stove to remove the cornbread just in the knick of time.

She turned the cast-iron pan upside down and flipped the cornbread onto a plate. Looking around, Teri saw a heap of corn in need of shucking. In no time at all, the sisters were working in a comfortable silence with one another, stealing glances without wanting to make any direct eye contact.

Bird chopped celery, Maxine put the cat-fish, seasoned to perfection, into the hot grease, and Teri removed the silk threads from the corn stalks.

The church bells rang. They all knew that meant service was over. Kenny entered from the TV room. He and Maxine looked at Ahmad, hoping that he would not be disappointed. His fingers were crossed, and he hoped that he would not be, either.

The silence was deafening as the dinner table was prepared. Maxine and Bird pulled the table from both ends and inserted the two table leaves to accommodate seating for eight. Teri placed a Battenburg tablecloth on top. Silverware was set, along with the napkins, dishes, and serving trays. Everything was in place when the doorbell rang.

"I'll get it," shouted Ahmad, who clearly wanted to play host. After all, it was his party. He raced to the door and his spirits were way up there with Big Mama in heaven. He kept thinking, I knew they'd come, I just knew it.

"Hey there, little man," Miles greeted as they knocked fists.

"Thanks for coming."

"No, thank you for inviting me," Miles said before he knew that he was not the only one there. Ahmad quickly closed the door. When Miles saw Teri, he knew he had been suckered. And so did Teri, who threw up her hands and marched off to the kitchen in a rage.

The doorbell rang again, and it was Lem.

"When did you get out of jail?" Ahmad whispered.

Lem pulled Ahmed into the TV room. "I fucked up bad, didn't I?" he asked Ahmad, who said nothing.

195

"How's Bird?"

"She's in the kitchen. Why don't you ask her?" was all Ahmad had to say. He knew when to keep his mouth shut.

"That looks like a family thing in there. I don't wanna butt in."

"Why not . . . you're family," he assured his uncle.

Those were the words Lem had sat in jail a week waiting to hear. The sound of them now had his mind wandering a mile a minute.

"Look Ahmad, I know I let you down an' I'm sorry," he managed to say. "I-I guess I just . . . I didn't beat on your auntie. I pushed her," he explained, "and that was bad enough. But I didn't hit her. I would never hit a woman . . . believe me?"

"C'mon man." Ahmad's inviting smile was a yard of forgiveness.

Bird entered the room, carrying items to be set on the table, when she saw Lem, "Sweetheart, when did you get home?" she quizzed, wondering if having Lem show up for dinner was a part of Ahmad's little plan as well.

"I love you," Lem said sincerely. "I fucked up."

Bird looked deep into his eyes and she knew that he was truly sorry, and so was she.

"I have something I want to tell you," she said excitedly.

The front door opened and Faith walked in, surprised to see everybody else there, too.

Bird was too through that Faith had been invited to come, "I can't believe she's here," she said, rolling her eyes at her cousin.

Faith did not move from the doorway. She felt safest near the exit. Ahmad finally came over to greet her.

"Why is everyone here, Ahmad?" she asked her little cousin.

"We're having a Sunday dinner," he announced happily.

"Sunday dinner?" she repeated, wondering about the money and was a Sunday dinner the requirement in order to be shown the cash?

"Yes, we have fried chicken, corn bread, dumplings—"

Faith furiously interrupted him, "Not cool, Ahmad. I'm leaving."

Ahmad looked sadly at her. "Please stay."

Maxine announced, "Dinner's served."

197

○　　○　　○

Bird and Maxine brought the food to the dining room table where the guests sat in silence. Teri sat away from Miles. Faith felt safest sitting between Reverend Williams and Kenny. No one knew what to say. No one had bothered to mend the broken pieces before that very moment. Not one of the adults had made the first step in the process of healing. When the table was filled to capacity, Ahmad led Lem to his seat as the final item to be placed.

Kenny whispered under his breath, "Please Lord, no shit today."

Lem avoided all eyes. Bird didn't know how to feel.

Lem's throat was dry and parched. His lips begged for water. He knew he needed to say something. He couldn't just stroll into the house, take his seat at the table, and not greet the family. He looked around his place setting for something to drink, but the Kool-Aid had yet to be poured.

Everybody was looking at him, waiting to see what he had to say. He swallowed hard, hoping it would bring a bit of relief to the desert at the back of his throat. "I-it's so good to see everybody again."

He and Bird exchanged loving looks, and her warm smile let him know she was really glad to see him.

Ahmad thought, Way to go, Uncle Lem, as he tapped his glass with his fork, turning the attention to himself before his crazy family put Lem on trial right there at the dinner family.

"Hey, Reverend Williams? Think I could bless the table this time?"

"Of course, young man."

Everybody was stunned that Ahmad had actually volunteered to pray, and heads bowed one at a time.

"Dear Lord, thank you for allowing us another day on Earth," he began with emotion. "Another day to glorify your holy name and sanctify ourselves with your mercy. Oh Lord, I am grateful that all the people I love most in the world are here to celebrate life and all the lessons we learn as it unfolds . . ."

Eyes all around the table begin to pop open. They were pleasantly surprised . . . Ahmad could preach!

". . . so let one of those lessons be acceptance and love. So that we can be a family again and love each other like we used to. In Christ Jesus's name . . . Amen."

"Amen," chimed all, just short of cheering for the beautiful prayer. Ahmad was congratulated with high fives and head rubs.

"I have a surprise for everyone later," Maxine teased. "But for now, let's eat."

"Amen to that!" agreed Reverend Williams.

Despite the momentary good feeling, tension was as thick as a fog rolling in from Lake Michigan. But that did not stop the ceremonial process of the consumption of food. Platters of chicken and fish, bowls of greens and turnips, baskets of cornbread and hotcakes were all passed in an awkward silence.

Miles and Faith separately tried to make eye contact with Ahmad, but he refused to look at them directly. He felt a bit guilty for what he had done, but for now, he did not care if they sat eating in silence. He only cared that they were together. He was as happy as he could have possibly been at that moment. So he ate his food quietly while he relished his family reunion.

The meal was excellent. It was evident by the way forks scraped against the china and the fried chicken was crunched. Finally, everyone laughed out loud at the quiet that magnified the sounds of their eating and the silliness of their silence.

When the roaring laughter calmed down, Lem had news he wanted to share. "I got my job back."

Congratulations came from the table all around.

"They asked me back 'cause they say I'm a good, strong, skilled worker."

"I know." Bird blushed.

Kenny asked between bites, "Hey how did you get out of jail, man?"

"To tell you the truth, man, I don't even know. My charges got dropped. Somebody talked to somebody . . . an' I don't know," he said happily. "Here I am."

"Well, we're glad to have you home, Lem," Maxine assured him.

"That's right, my Boo is home," Bird gushed, rubbing his leg.

Lem beamed.

Teri piped up, "Actually, *I* called my friend at the DA's office for a favor. *That's* how you got out." She didn't want him confused.

"I felt bad," she said sheepishly to Bird, who was happy she helped.

Lem was mad. "Well, you should feel bad. Because of you, I had to spend a week in jail."

"You should be thankful I helped you out," she told him flippantly. Instead of letting it go with that, she added, "Now you can take care of your pregnant wife."

Lem's fork dropped to his plate and his mouth to the floor as he turned completely to look at Bird in shock.

Bird could have slapped Teri to East Giblip. "You know what, Teri, you really need to mind your own damn business. Didn't nobody ask you for no help. You need to be worried about your own husband and why he's sleeping with Faith."

That bit of news sent another shock wave through Lem, and he snapped his head from Bird's attention toward Miles. "Damn," he mouthed in disbelief. Lem had wanted to know what was going on in the family while he was gone. He knew all he had to do was keep his seat, because in a moment or two, he was about to find out all the details.

Miles stopped eating. Bird's comment struck him way deep.

Faith stood to leave. She didn't want to be the focus of another inquisition.

"No, Faith, sit," Maxine ordered.

"She can go if she wants, Max," Teri shouted back, hoping she would leave.

"Oh, no," Maxine said to Faith, "you don't need to run away again. You're family and we're gonna work this out. Faith," she said, pointing to the chair for her to sit.

Maxine could see things getting ugly. "Baby, why don't you go and get some peas. And take your sister with you," she ordered, handing Ahmad the bowl and tending to the baby in the bassinet next to her.

Ahmad's smile had disappeared. A look of dismay covered his little face. His plan had fallen completely apart. You can't depend on these adults for shit, he thought as he stomped off to the kitchen with Kelly.

When the kids were out of range, Teri glared into her husband's eyes. "Was that it, Miles, huh? I didn't take care of you?" she questioned him directly.

"We haven't been happy for a long time," said Miles sadly as he shook his head.

He looked around the table at the people who had become like his own family to him. He was reluctant to have such a conversation about one of their very own in front of them.

"We used to have so much fun together." He smiled as he remembered.

Teri looked down at her plate sadly. "I don't know what happened. I just always lose what I love," she said, looking into Miles's eyes, suddenly recognizing the truth about herself. Losing anything had Teri so paralyzed that she closed herself down to all possibilities. Her eyes brimmed with tears.

There was not even an ice cube rattling—everyone was stark still. Ahmad had to be extra careful so he wouldn't get caught eavesdropping. He knew that since it was so quiet in there he had better move around in the kitchen. He searched for a spoon and put some peas into the bowl. Trying to listen to his plan bombing bigtime out there, he poured way too many peas and spilled them all over his hands.

"Well, good luck with Mama Joe's money," Miles said, standing to leave.

"Mother Joe's money?" Maxine asked. "What are y'all talkin' about?"

Bird explained, "Well, supposedly Mama has all of this money stashed somewhere here in the house, and she was saving it for Ahmad. That's why we're all here today."

This was the first Maxine had heard of this, and she didn't like it. "Ahmad, get in here!"

"Ahmad!" Kenny echoed.

He had heard the conversation turning his way, and he panicked. Grabbing a towel, he wiped his hands and the bottom of the bowl, absentmindedly tossed the towel on the stove, and casually walked into the dining room. Ahmad sheepishly appeared with the peas and sat the bowl in front of Reverend Williams.

Kenny crossed his arms. "Where is this money Mother Joe supposedly left you?"

"There isn't any money," he answered the family teary-eyed. "I made it all up."

The table exploded . . .

"You what!"

"No you didn't!"

"How could you lie!"

"Aw, come on!"

"Made it all up!" Maxine screamed. "Boy, what have I told you about lying?"

Ahmad hung his head, and the family started to argue among themselves. He could not control the tears that spilled onto his face. He was fed up with the bickering.

"It's all y'alls fault! Y'all messed up the family! Can't you see that!" he screamed above everybody, finally exploding. The built-up emotion he had been carrying around tumbled out all at once.

"Big Mama wanted me to get everyone together again for a Sunday dinner. But I didn't know how to do that, because all y'all do is fight!" he explained, breaking down each and every reason for his scheme.

"So I lied. Lied about the money so you'd come. So we could be a family again. Y'all know that's what Big Mama wanted," he appealed, sobbing.

There wasn't a dry eye in the room. Guilt touched every adult at the table. Maxine comforted her son and rocked him.

The dish towel's threads on the kitchen stove had caught fire and was engulfed in flames. The flames raced up the tile behind the stove and onto the wall and curtains.

"Hey, y'all smell that?" Kenny asked.

Everybody sniffed the air.

"It smells like it's coming from the kitchen," Miles said.

"Let's see what's goin' on in there," Kenny said as an order for the men in the house.

Maxine asked the kids, "Y'all didn't mess with the stove did you?" They shook their heads no way.

They opened the kitchen door to find flames galore.

"Oh shit!" Kenny screamed just as the smoke alarm blared.

"Somebody move the baby!" Maxine yelled.

Grabbing pots of water from the sink, Miles threw water onto the flames. It did nothing. The sound from the alarm was deafening. Everybody ran into the kitchen to help. Lem filled another pot of water. Reverend Williams entered with sopping wet towels and started beating down the flames. Bird kept the kids back while everyone threw water and beat at the flames.

The fire spread to an adjoining wall and panic spread.

"Where is the extinguisher?" Teri asked as she and Bird searched. They found two that Kenny and Miles used to kill the spreading fire.

"Move out of the way," Miles yelled to the ladies as they extinguished the remaining flames.

The piercing sound of the smoke alarm finally died. Lem turned on the large exhaust fan to draw out some of the smoke. Everyone stood in the kitchen with their own thoughts about how their family had come to such a crossroads. They knew the answer. Everybody looked at one another sadly as they inspected the damage.

Maxine picked up a dish towel on the stove that was burned and figured that the fire had started there.

Ahmad looked at the towel and remembered the words of Big Mama, "Never put a towel on the stove. You could burn the house down baby . . ." He could not have felt any worse. Not only had he lied to get everybody to dinner, but he burned down the kitchen just as Big Mama had warned.

The kitchen door burst open, scaring everyone. An old man wearing an black suit and carrying a small black-and-white TV ran in screaming, "Fire! Fire! Fire!" He was running back and forth to each person, wondering why everybody was just standing there.

Lem grabbed the fire extinguisher from Miles and sprayed the intruder with it to calm him down.

Getting a closer look, Maxine could see that it was Uncle Pete. "Uncle Pete! Stop!" she said, taking his hand. "The fire's out. Uncle Pete was my surprise," she said to the others.

"*This* is crazy-ass Uncle Pete?" Lem asked.

Uncle Pete still wanted to leave the house. Where he came from, when a fire alarm rang, you were supposed to grab what valuables you could and get out. So he pulled away from Maxine so he could leave and dropped the small TV. It broke into tiny pieces, exposing green paper stuffed inside the TV's back cover.

Taking a closer look, everyone could see that it was money—and lots of it. The automatic fan in the kitchen not only circulated the fresh air, but it blew the dollars into swirls above their heads. There were fives, tens, and twenties floating everywhere in abundance. They all began to laugh while reaching for the floating bills.

Teri felt terrible. She went to Ahmad and tried to console him, wiping his tears. She cried with her nephew, and it felt good.

Maxine walked toward the two crying. "Teri, I'm your sister. And I love you." She cried, hugging Teri.

"I'm sorry, too, sis," Teri cried, hugging back.

"Teri, thanks for getting me out," Lem said. He reached for a hug from Teri as well.

An air of healed wounds began to circulate from one person to another. I'm *sorry*s and *I love you*s came freely to the Joseph family's lips. They had been through a series of long and painful ordeals, and the heat of the fire had finally burned away the pain.

209

Lem snuck up behind Bird and rubbed her belly, letting her know he was pleased with the news. She fell into his arms crying, happy that he approved.

Reverend Williams stood back and mused, "This is better than *All My Children*."

Maxine and Teri found each other again for another round of hugs. Maxine was really touched. Teri had never called her "sis." She felt good to have her big sister back for real.

Teri had been the only one who thought to ask the old man details about what was in back of the TV. "Uncle Pete, whose money is this?"

"Joe's money!" he said matter-of-factly, tossing up a handful. "Mother Joe's money!"

So it wasn't a myth, there really was money. Mother Joe did hate banks. If money was stuffed in the TV, there had to be more around the house somewhere, Ahmad figured, and started laughing loudly. He could not control himself. Soon, everyone else was doubled over with laughter, too. The fact that there really was money had them in hysterics at the irony of it all.

Ahmad looked around the room at his family, who began to put their lives back together even without Mother Joe. He finally understood what soul food and Sunday dinners meant to the black family.

During slavery, black folks didn't have choices in life, so cooking became a way to share feelings and love and to nurture family. Dinners were a time to share happiness and sorrow, unity and strength, things the old folks say is missing in today's families . . .

Some of the families' most difficult problems were brought to and solved at the dinner table. Ahmad saw now that his family was no different.

THE FOLLOWING SPRING, THE JOSEPH FAMILY happily worked together in Mother Joe's garden. It was time for the garden to be turned over and seeds to be planted for the summer's harvest. They planted tomatoes, greens, corn, carrots, and all types of roses and herbs.

The Sunday dinner tradition continued and thrived. Their family focus collectively switched to "we."

Mother Joe would have been proud.

○   ○   ○

By summer, the garden was in full bloom. With the combination of vegetables, flowers, and herbs, it had an aroma all of its own. No wonder Mother Joe loved her garden so much. Ahmad, Teri, Maxine, and Bird plucked the fresh items from the ground, cleaned some for dinner, and divided the lot between them.

Ahmad was pleased to see such an easy comfort between his mom and her sisters as they laughed and joked around. Uncle Pete sat in the yard in his rocker, watching and doling out orders. Lem, Kenny, and Miles played a game of basketball in the yard. Ah yes, he smiled to himself, his little plan had worked after all.

Things certainly got better for the Joseph family. Even though Miles and Teri got a divorce, it didn't stop Miles from coming around every now and then to fill his belly with Maxine's soul food and see the folks he had known for so long.

Lem and Bird were happy together and had their own place. They were expecting their first child any day.

The house was taken off the market, and Maxine and Teri were buddies with one another again. Faith, finally, was part of the family, too.

Though they grieved the death of Mother Joe, there was a feeling of completion, because she had done everything she had set out to do—to build a strong family with a rich tradition and to leave love in her footprints.

Ahmad walked the yard, looking at everyone enjoying themselves with each other. He held a rose from the garden as a testament to the growth and nourishment of their souls that Mother Joe had provided for the family.

The rose he held was a fruit of his deed, and he was proud of the beauty that his labor had yielded. Ahmad closed his eyes and said, "Thanks, Big Mama . . ." as he took a whiff of the rose's sweet scent, inhaling deep the memories that he would cherish forever.

A collection of recipes for a soul
food feast from the *Soul Food* family

Nia Long
CRAB CAKES
Serves 4

1   egg
2   tablespoons mayonnaise
½   teaspoon dry mustard
⅛   teaspoon ground hot red pepper
    (cayenne)
¼   teaspoon Tabasco sauce
½   teaspoon salt
½   teaspoon pepper
1   pound fresh crabmeat, cleaned and
    drained
3   tablespoons finely chopped fresh parsley
1 ½ tablespoons bread crumbs
    Vegetable oil for frying
1   lemon, cut into wedges
Tartar sauce

Beat egg lightly with whisk. Add mayonnaise, mustard, red pepper, Tabasco, salt, and pepper until mixture is smooth. Add crabmeat, parsley, and bread crumbs, and toss with a fork. Divide mixture into 8 equal portions about 2 to 2 ½ inches in diameter. Wrap in wax paper for 30 minutes. Chill.

Deep-fry crab cakes, four at a time, until golden brown. Drain on paper towels. Arrange crab cake with lemon wedges and serve with Tartar sauce.

Irma P. Hall
MAMA PLAYER'S LOUISIANA SALMON CROQUETTES

Serves 4

1	can red salmon
1	yellow onion, chopped fine
1	bell pepper
2	slices bread
1	medium white potato, boiled and mashed
1	egg
1	teaspoon black pepper

Yellow cornmeal

Combine first seven ingredients until well blended. Shape into patties. Coat in cornmeal and fry in hot oil, turning once. Lay on paper towels to drain. Serve hot.

Gina Ravera
BALITAS DE BACALAO
(Codfish Balls)

1   pound dried codfish
1   cup mashed potatoes
2   cloves garlic, crushed
1   small onion, minced
1 ½ tablespoons minced fresh parsley
4   large eggs, separated
1   cup fine bread crumbs
1   tablespoon salted butter
vegetable or peanut oil for frying

Soak salted cod fish in water overnight. Drain fish and place in a small saucepan and cover with cold water. Bring to a boil over medium/high heat. Simmer over medium/low heat for 15–20 minutes until tender. Drain fish when cool, then skin, remove bones, and flake the fish.

Mix flaked cod fish, mashed potatoes, egg yolks, onion, garlic, parsley, and seasoning together in a large bowl and stir well. Set aside.

Sprinkle a layer of bread crumbs on a plate or cutting board. Roll mixture into small balls. Roll balls in the crumbs, renewing crumbs when necessary.

Heat 4–5 inches of oil in a large, heavy saucepan (must be hot enough so that a drop of batter sizzles when dropped in the oil). Fry the balls a few at a time, until golden brown, for 3–5 minutes.

Remove balls from pan with a slotted spoon and drain on paper towels.

Serve warm and enjoy.

Vanessa Williams
STUFFED PEPPERS

10   small green peppers
3   tablespoons oil
1   medium onion
$\frac{1}{2}$ pound ground beef
$\frac{1}{2}$ pound ground pork
$\frac{1}{2}$ cup rice
1   teaspoon salt
$\frac{1}{2}$ teaspoon pepper
1   egg
2   small cans tomato sauce

Wash peppers, cut off tops, remove seeds, and scrape with a spoon. Mince and brown onion in oil, pour into bowl, and add meat, washed rice, salt, pepper, and beaten egg. Mix well. Fill each green pepper almost to the top with mixture. Place peppers into deep pot. Pour on tomato sauce and enough water to cover. Simmer for about 1 hour or until rice is cooked.

Recipe by Sylvia A. King

Gina Ravera
Arroz con Pollo
(Chicken and Rice)

One 3-pound chicken, cut into 8 pieces and
    skin removed
2   teaspoons salt
Freshly ground pepper to taste
juice of one lime
½   cup pure Spanish olive oil
2   medium onions, finely chopped
3–4 cloves of garlic, minced
1   teaspoon ground cumin
1   bay leaf
½   cup dry white wine
5   cups chicken broth
1   14-ounce package or 1 1/2 cups of short-
    grain rice, soaked for 1 hour in cold water
1   cup drained sweet peas
2   pimentos, chopped for garnish

Wash chicken, pat dry, and sprinkle with salt, pepper, and lime juice.

In a large, heavy casserole pan over medium heat, heat ¼ cup of oil. Lower heat, being careful not to burn the oil, add the chicken and one of the two chopped onions. Brown.

Remove chicken and browned onions from oil and set aside. Discard burnt onion particles. Add

continued on page 224

remaining oil to dish and cook second onion with garlic, stirring until onion is transparent, 6–8 minutes. Add cumin and bay leaf. Stir until well mixed. Add chicken, stir well, and add wine. Cook for 5 minutes.

Add stock and bring to a boil. Add salt to taste (plus a bit extra, since the rice will absorb the salt later). Add drained rice.

Preheat oven to 350 degrees.

Bring dish to a boil over high heat and cook uncovered until most of the water has been absorbed and small craters form on top of the rice, 20–25 minutes.

Remove from heat. Add $3/4$ cup of peas, cover and place in oven until rice is tender, about 20 minutes (add more water if necessary). Rice can also be cooked on the stove, but is more tender when cooked in oven.

Transfer to a serving platter. Garnish with remaining peas and pimentos.

Vivica A. Fox
SMOTHERED AND COVERED CHOPS

4–8   beef or pork chops
½   cup of milk whipped with one egg
garlic salt and black pepper
1   cup of flour, flavored with Lawry's
    seasoning salt
1½   cups of peanut oil
1   white onion, chopped
1   bell pepper, chopped
8–10 mushrooms, sliced
½   stick of butter
1½   cups of cold water

Dip chops into milk and egg batter. Then sprinkle with garlic salt and black pepper. Coat battered chops with flour and seasoning salt. Fry chops in hot peanut oil until golden brown.

Sauté chopped onion, bell pepper, and mushrooms in butter and garlic salt.

With leftover peanut oil, start to make gravy. Sprinkle ½ cup of flour (more if needed) into 4 tablespoons of oil to make gravy base. With a fork stir into smooth brown paste. Add 1½–2 cups of cold water. Bring to a boil, stirring occasionally. Add sautéed vegetables, cook for 15–20 minutes. Add golden brown chops. Simmer over low heat for 10–15 minutes.

Serves 4.

George Tillman, Jr.
FRIED CORN
Serves 8

½   pound fat back or salt pork
10–12 ears of corn
½   cup flour
1   tablespoon salt
1   teaspoon black pepper
4   cups water

Cut meat into small slices and parboil (to get the salt out). Then cook as you would bacon. Drain the fat into a large skillet.

Shuck the corn, pick out as many of the silks as possible. Wash corn in cold water, cut from the cob in small cuts (go around each ear twice, then scrap the cob). Mix together flour, salt, pepper, and water. Add corn and mix well. Pour into hot skillet and cook at low to medium heat for an hour, stirring often. If corn gets too dry, add a little more water. If you like, you can add a few slices of the meat into the corn while it's cooking.

Tracey Edmonds
MACARONI AND CHEESE

3   cups of macaroni
1 ½ cups of grated cheese (or more,
      depending on your taste)
½   stick of butter
1   cup milk
1   egg
Salt
Pepper

Preheat oven to 350°.

Place macaroni in pot of water (add a pinch of salt) and boil until tender. Drain.

In a long, 2-inch casserole dish, layer macaroni. Add salt and pepper with bits of butter. Add a layer of grated cheese over the macaroni. Continue layering in the same pattern, ending with cheese on top.

In a separate bowl, mix 1 cup of milk and 1 beaten egg together with salt and pepper. Pour mixture over macaroni and cheese.

Place in oven and bake until cheese has melted and milk mixture is cooked.

Vivica A. Fox
VIVICA'S MARVELOUS MACARONI

1   box of elbow macaroni
2   cans of cream of mushroom soup
1   cup of milk
1   cube of shredded cheddar cheese
fresh black pepper
sprinkles of Accent salt
2   eggs
½   stick of butter, melted
1   capful of olive oil

Boil noodles, then drain. Mix the milk and eggs together in a pot over medium heat. Bring to a slight boil, then add cream of mushroom soup and bring to a medium boil. Add salt and pepper. Add sauce to sautéed butter and oil. Grease casserole dish, add cooked noodles and sauce. Bake at 375 degrees for 30–45 minutes. Sprinkle with shredded cheddar cheese, then cook for 10 more minutes. Turn oven to low and cook for 10 more minutes.

Serves 6 to 8.

Kenny Edmonds
FRIED CABBAGE

1   head of cabbage
6   strips of bacon
Butter
Salt

Shred cabbage and remove center. Place cabbage in pot of water and bring to a boil. Add pinch of salt. Drain cabbage.

In skillet, fry bacon. When done, put to the side and crumble on a separate plate. With leftover bacon drippings, fry cabbage. Add one tablespoon of butter.

Add crumbled bacon to cabbage and simmer for 5 minutes.

Bob Teitel
MYRTA'S SLAMMIN'
POTATO SALAD

10	pounds Idaho potatoes
12	hard-boiled eggs, chopped fine
4	large carrots, chopped fine
3	cups chopped celery
1	cup green scallions
2	16-ounce jars Miracle Whip
1	teaspoon paprika
4	tablespoons sour cream

Salt and pepper

Peel and boil potatoes until tender. Drain and let cool. Chop into cubes. Add remaining ingredients and mix together. Chill for 3 hours before serving.

George Tillman, Jr.
MOM'S COLLARD GREENS

3   bunches collard greens
2   ham hocks
1 ½ tablespoons salt
Hot peppers

Clean greens with a towel and break off all long stems. Stack with larger green leaves on the bottom. When you have a sizable stack, roll tightly and cut into ¼ inch strips.

Wash in the sink, changing water until greens are completely clean. Place in pot, fill about ⅔ full with water, let come to a boil, and continue boiling for 10 minutes. Drain, refill with same amount of water, add ham hocks and salt, and cook until greens and ham hock are tender, approximately 3 hours. Add hot pepper to taste and let simmer for 10 to 15 minutes.

LaJoyce Brookshire
LAJOYCE'S MEATLESS MEAN GREENS

2   pounds collard greens
2   tablespoons Lawry's Seasoned Salt
¼   cup hot sauce
1   teaspoon chopped garlic
¼   teaspoon garlic powder
2   packages of Goya's Jamon Seasoning
1   tablespoon sugar
2   tablespoons olive oil

Fill an 8-quart pot almost to the top with water.

Add all ingredients except collard greens, sugar and olive oil, and bring to a rapid boil.

While water is boiling clean greens and shred finely, adding them bit by bit to the boiling water.

Once all of the greens are added, keep pot at a rapid boil with the top off for about 45 minutes. Greens should be tender, not mushy.

When most of the water has boiled down low, add sugar and olive oil.

Cover pot and leave on stove overnight or throughout the day to allow seasonings to saturate.

Refrigerate for a few hours before reheating and serving with hot cornbread.

Vanessa Williams
SPRITE POUND CAKE

3   cups sugar
3   sticks margarine or butter
6   eggs
3   cups flour
¾   cups Sprite
3   teaspoons lemon flavoring

Cream sugar and margarine until smooth. Add one egg at a time and beat. Add flour and stir. Combine Sprite and lemon flavoring and mix into batter until smooth. Bake at 325° in loaf pan for 1 hour.

Recipe by Willie Warmly

Michael Beach
DOCE DE PAPAYA VERDE RALADA COM MEL
(Sweet of Grated Green Papaya with Honey)

1   green papaya
    equal quantity of honey
    fig leaves

Peel, wash, and grate the green papaya. Measure the same quantity of honey and cook with the papaya and fig leaves over moderate heat until it thickens and a spoon drawn across the bottom leaves a clean path. As a variation, cut the papayas into very fine strips and proceed in the same manner.

Nia Long
PEACH COBBLER

Filling: 3 tablespoons cornstarch
$\frac{1}{2}$ cup sugar
Ground cloves, nutmeg, cinnamon
2 large (24-ounce) cans of sliced peaches in heavy syrup
1 grated lemon peel
Juice from lemon
$\frac{1}{2}$ stick butter

Crust: 1 tablespoon orange juice
$\frac{2}{3}$ cup shortening ($\frac{1}{2}$ Crisco and $\frac{1}{2}$ butter)
2 cups all-purpose flour
1 teaspoon salt
6 tablespoons frozen orange juice concentrate
1 egg white
$\frac{1}{2}$ stick butter

Stir together cornstarch, sugar, and spices. Add peaches. Add lemon peel, juice, and butter. Cook over medium heat until thick.

Dilute orange juice with water, but leave fairly thick. Mix butter and Crisco with flour, and add orange juice mixture. Work flour mixture and roll out.

Place peach mixture into pie pan and cover with crust. Melt $\frac{1}{2}$ stick butter with tablespoon of orange juice. Whisk in egg white. Brush on pie. Sprinkle generous amounts of sugar on top. Bake at 425° for about 30 minutes.

Jeffrey D. Sams
APPLE PIE

Filling: 6–7 apples (any variety, depending on taste)
⅔ cup sugar
½ cup water
1 teaspoon cinnamon
1 teaspoon nutmeg or 1 teaspoon vanilla extract
1 teaspoon cornstarch
Crust: 1 stick Crisco, butter flavor
Flour
Water

Peel apples and place in pot. Add sugar, spices, and cornstarch/water mixture. Cook until apples are tender, but not quite done.

In a separate bowl, mash Crisco. Add flour until it looks like coarse corn meal, adding a little water at a time until mixture doesn't stick to your hands. Roll out dough and place it in pie pan.

Pour apples over dough. With the remaining dough, cut strips and arrange in crisscross pattern over tops of apples. Bake at 350° until crust is brown, about 30 to 45 minutes.

Michael Beach
COFFEE PUDDING
(Fogo Island)

1   large glass of milk
1   large glass of strong coffee
1   pound of sugar
12 egg yolks
1   teaspoon of corn starch

Make a syrup with coffee and sugar. Set aside a small portion to cover the bottom of the pan. Let the rest of coffee syrup cool off, and mix in the yolks, milk, and corn starch. Strain and cook in a double boiler until thick. Remove from heat and serve either at room temperature or chilled.

Recipe by Vina Vieira Martins

Irma P. Hall
AUNT BEA'S CARMEL CANDY

2   cups sugar
2   cups cream (not canned)
1 ¾ cups white Karo syrup
1   cup butter
1   pinch salt

Combine all ingredients, except 1 cup of cream, in a medium saucepan. Boil for 30 minutes until thick, then add second cup of cream. Cook to 248° using candy thermometer. Optional: Add nuts of choice.

Pour candy into buttered 4 x 4-inch pan. Let cool and harden. Cut into squares.

Brandon Hammond
SWEET POTATO PIE

2–4 sweet potatoes or yams
1   stick butter or margarine
2   eggs
2   cups of sugar (more if you like your pies really sweet)
1   14-ounce can of condensed milk
1   cup flour
2   tablespoons baking powder
Ground cinnamon to taste
Ground nutmeg to taste
1   tablespoon vanilla extract
1   9-inch unbaked pastry shell

Peel potatoes/yams, cut into sections, and boil till tender. Drain. In large bowl, mix potatoes, eggs, butter, and sugar until smooth. Slowly add milk and flour (alternating between the two). Add baking powder, cinnamon, nutmeg, and vanilla. If necessary, continue adding sugar, cinnamon, and nutmeg to taste, being careful not to overseason. Batter should be smooth and easy to pour.

Pour into pastry shell and bake at 425° for 35–45 minutes or until edges of pastry shell are golden brown. Let stand until mixture has hardened enough to cut. Serve with ice cream or eat alone. Refrigerate leftovers.

Mekhi Pfifer
SWEET POTATO PIE

1   pound sweet potatoes
¾   cup sugar
1   teaspoon cinnamon
½   teaspoon nutmeg
salt
¼   teaspoon vanilla extract
2   drops lemon flavoring
2   eggs, lightly beaten
1   can evaporated milk
½   cup of regular milk
pie crust
whipped cream

Boil sweet potatoes until soft. In a large mixing bowl, combine sweet potatoes, sugar, cinnamon, nutmeg, a pinch of salt, ½ teaspoon vanilla extract, lemon flavoring, and eggs. Slowly add evaporated milk and regular milk and mix well.

Pour into pastry-lined pie pan. Cover edge of pie crust with foil. Bake at 375 for 25 minutes. Remove foil and bake for 25–30 minutes or more, until knife comes out clean. Serve with whipped cream.

Jeffrey D. Sams
BANANA PUDDING

1   box lemon pudding and pie filling
1   lemon
1   box vanilla wafers
3   ripe bananas

Make lemon pudding as directed on box. When thickened, squeeze lemon juice and grate lemon rind into pudding. Mix well.

Arrange vanilla wafers so that they cover the bottom of a flat-bottomed glass bowl. Pour pudding to cover cookies, then layer sliced bananas on top of that. Repeat layers until ingredients are gone.

Refrigerate and serve when chilled.

LaJoyce Brookshire
GRANNIE'S COCONUT CAKE

½ pound butter
2 cups sugar
4 eggs
1 ½ teaspoons pure vanilla extract
1 teaspoon lemon extract
1 teaspoon baking powder
2 cups cake flour
1 cup milk
A pinch of salt
1 bag Baker's coconut
1 jar pineapple preserves
low-fat vanilla icing

Do the following by hand: Combine softened butter and sugar until creamy. Add sugar and blend well. Fold in eggs one by one, then add extracts. Sift in cake flour, baking powder and salt, adding one cup of flour at a time. Add milk and continue to mix by hand until smooth.

Use a hand mixer for 2 minutes on medium speed.

Pour cake mix into 2 greased and floured 9 cake pans.

Bake at 350° until golden brown.

Frosting: Spread pineapple preserves on the first cake layer thickly. Place the other layer on top and put preserves all over top. On the sides put low-fat vanilla icing. Finally add coconut all over.

Warning . . . Don't hurt yourself.